More Aster(ix) Anthologies

Best of Hot Metal Bridge
April 2021

The Ferrante Project
October 2020

The Poetry Issue
Winter 2020

Inheritance
Summer 2019

(Un)bound [double issue]
Winter 2018/2019

as well as...

Edges - Fall 2018

Dirty Laundry - Fall 2017

Kitchen Table Translation - Summer 2017

Best of Kweli - Spring 2017

What We Love - Fall 2016

Atravesando - Spring 2016

and more!

available for order wherever books are sold

and don't forget to visit
asterixjournal.com
for more content and information

Aster(ix) Journal
www.asterixjournal.com

Editor-in-chief/Founder
Angie Cruz

Publisher/Founder
Adriana E. Ramírez

Senior Editor
Tanya Shirazi

Managing Editor
Amanda Tien

Contributing Editors to
The Fiction Issue
Bianca Hernandez
Paola Liendo
Aeriel Merillat

Contributing Editors
Rosa Alcalá, Arielle
Greenberg, Yona Harvey,
Daisy Hernandez, J. A. Howard,
Sheila Maldonado, Dawn
Lundy Martin, Oindrila
Mukherjee, Idra Novey,
Emily Raboteau, Nelly Rosario,
Zohra Saed, Sun Yung Shin,
Jenelle Troxell, Chika Unigwe,
Marta Lucía Vargas, Autumn
Womack, Elleni Centime Zeleke

Advisory Editors
Ari Ariel, Armando Garcia,
Amy Sara Carroll, Norma
Cantú, Xochi Candalaria,
Jennifer Clement, Edwidge
Danticat, Cristina García,
Stephanie Elizondo Griest,
Andrea Thome, Helena Maria
Viramontes

Aster(ix) print issues are usually published 2-3 times a year in print with additional content online. **Aster(ix)** is funded in part by the Dietrich School of Arts and Sciences and the Department of English at University of Pittsburgh.

Aster(ix) Journal

presents

The Fiction Issue

Edited by
Ayşe Papatya Bucak & Ivelisse Rodriguez, PhD

December 2021

BLUE SKETCH PRESS | PITTSBURGH

Cecilia Vicuña Explanation: *Amaranta*
Oil on canvas, 1972-2021
As written in *Catalogue for Shanghai Biennale*, **2021**

A girl is wrapped in her menstruation as if it were a gown of blood. Because her menstruation is perceived as a disgusting threat, a man knifes her laughing gaudily as he murders her, while another man laughs even harder, holding her wrap of blood that now is a prison tethering her to bone poles. A telephone line controls her and two hands, male and female, push her in place to facilitate the murder.

Cecilia Vicuña Explicación: *Amaranta*
óleo sobre lienzo, 1972-2021
Como escrito en el *Catalogue for Shanghai Biennale*, **2021**

Una niña está envuelta en su menstruación como si fuera un vestido de sangre. Debido a que su menstruación se percibe como una amenaza repugnante, un hombre la apuñala riendose alegremente al asesinarla, mientras que otro hombre se ríe aún más fuerte, sosteniendo el vestido de sangre que ahora es una prisión amarrándola a postes de hueso. Una línea telefónica la controla y dos manos, masculinas y femeninas, la empujan para facilitar el asesinato.

Contents

LETTERS FROM THE EDITORS

Ayşe Papatya Bucak & Ivelisse Rodriguez, PhD

When Zadie Smith published her short story "Two Men Arrive in a Village" in The New Yorker, she said in an interview that her goal was to write a short story that was both specific and universal. She said, "I started thinking of all the ways the local and specific enable one kind of engagement and potentially block another, particularly when you're talking about violence. 'Oh, that's just what happens in Africa,' or 'Well, Eastern Europe has always been like that.' Sometimes the specific details allows us to hold certain situations at a distance. [It] made me wonder: Is it possible to write a story that happens in many places at many times simultaneously? That implicates everybody?"

Smith wanted to place "Two Men Arrive in a Village," a story about military men assaulting village women, into a context that was not without time and place, but rather was in every time and place. In so doing, Smith made clear just how big a short story can be.

I think sometimes writers conflate short stories with small stories. Stories have to be focused and quick, critics seem to suggest. But what I love about short stories is just how big they can be within a small space. How they can implicate everybody while being about somebody.

The stories in this issue of Aster(ix) are big stories told in small spaces, by writers from all over the world. They are also, like Smith's story, both specific and universal.

Their individual similes and metaphors may be different—

take "Baby is beautiful. Like a slab of soft butter, a jar of clear ghee" from "Lina and Baby" by Amy Olassa

or "… their laughter, thin and sugary as capulin jam…" from "Snap This Photo of Two Good Men" by Catalina Bartlett

or "This was you shouting big, squeezing all your face into one tight ball like you ate too much impwa" from "Last-Last Resignation" by Mubanga Kalimamukwento

or finally "Since last Sunday's dinner at Sue's, I couldn't stop thinking about strawberry shortcake. Soft crumbly bread the color of lotus petals and strawberry bits somehow made sweeter by smooth white cream have made even runny eggs in soy sauce pale in comparison." from "Today I will Bake A Cake" by Layhannara Tep

—that is to say, each cultural setting may be different--but the feelings and relationships and rites of passage evoked by each story are shared by so many humans across the globe.

In my experience, readers tend to be one of two types: those who wish to see their own experiences in the stories they read and those who wish to see experiences previously unknown to them in the stories they read. I'm a reader who wants both—to recognize my shared humanity in the characters and to enter a life I have not myself lived.

These authors take us to settings as far ranging as a Chinese cemetery in Jamaica in "The Bank of Paradise" by Monique McIntosh, a grocery store in Beaverton, Oregon and a Cambodian refugee camp in "Today I Will Bake a Cake," a beauty salon in India in "Lina and Baby," and a Turkish prison in Sabahattin Ali's "The Wall". While each of these places was new to me, the range of emotions exhibited by the characters were not. There's been lots of talk over the years about how literature teaches us to feel empathy for other people, but what each of these stories really teach us is there is no such thing as other people, there is only us.

—Ayşe Papatya Bucak

Dear Short Story,

I won't write you love letters because you don't need love letters. I know, you can't seem to shake your negative rep: "no one likes you, you're only good for workshop, no one wants to buy you." It's hard living in a world where you are forever second best. (I know how that feels!) You had your heyday in the 14th century with *One Thousand and One Nights* and *The Canterbury Tales*. It's in the 17th and 18th centuries where the novel was the most popular girl in the world. But you came back for your crown in the 18th and 19th centuries. But the damn big, curvaceous novel always seems to best you. She sure knows how to seduce!

You may have spent a lot of time going to self-help seminars, shouting from the sidelines, having people speak on your behalf, trying to figure out how to make your detractors love you. But, oh, short story, you can't make people love you. As I once wrote, "what must be cajoled will never stay." You can't convince people of your worth.

So, it's not for you to change how the world sees you; it's not for you to carry a chip on your shoulder, a megaphone at your lips, always trying to show how you are good enough. You have no control over that.

It's for you to step out of the novel's shadow. You don't need to stand next to anybody who takes all your shine. You have your own spotlight to bloom under that is not predicated on comparison but is predicated on your sole existence. People like to create drama: #TeamShortStory or #TeamNovel. But you don't need each other to exist, and you don't to be pitted against each other. Like Paul D said to Sethe: "You your best thing."

Just take a look at the stories in this collection. What you hold in your hands is the world; these stories allow us to traverse countries and continents, dive into familial love or love woes, and yearn for and arrive at freedom. And that is your best thing.

Ivelisse Rodriguez, PhD
Guest Editor

Time Wave

Racquel Goodinson

Gilbert hit. I weighed 85 pounds. It was devastating. It took almost all the trees down. What the flood didn't wash away, damage, ruin, break and cause to rot, the 80 miles an hour winds uprooted and threw into the sea, the river, the street, the houses, the gullies and the fields. I was just glad that people had something else to fuss over other than my bones, my knees being bigger than my thighs, my veins showing blue through my skin pressed tight across my bones. Now they had to worry about the water muddy with sewage, their homes being damaged so badly they had no roofs to cover them and the mosquitoes being everywhere, spreading diseases like malaria and dengue and some said AIDS but no one knew for sure. It was the fall of 1988.

They walked through the tree littered streets in old dirty clothes and muddy sneakers. Their hair was uncombed. It sat on their heads in pink and yellow and green giant plastic rollers under tight mesh scarves. Or it sat in dusty clumps, all thirsty kinks and knots. Or it lay limp and dull on their head until an absent-minded hand ran through it quickly.

Mine was gone, wiped clean from my head with my father's shears. It was September 11th, the day before the hurricane, and I was 88 pounds. I couldn't stop. I knew it when I got off the scale and I knew it when I washed my thinning hair in the shower. I couldn't stop. So I ran the shears over my scalp, over and over again. And when the storm came, I was bald. But it was the least of everybody's trouble.

Things were bad everywhere.

This was the year I was set to graduate. This was the year that I had to take nine O levels and pass so that I could graduate. I was sixteen. It was heavy on me. But when the storm came it was something else to think about. I went to bed bald with the radio running on with warnings. Batten up. Winds in excess… Flood warnings… Head on hit. I slept like a worn out child.

In the morning no one mentioned my bald head. I ate a peg of grapefruit for breakfast. The ackee and salt fish and festivals went untouched. My mother wanted to know how I could possibly sleep. The zinc roof was ripped from the living room and half the house was flooded. The dogs were almost killed when the plum tree crashed into the backyard. And I slept, dead to the world. There was a storm like she'd never seen in all her years beating the island. She wanted to know how I could possibly sleep. I ran my hand over my clean head and said nothing.

The ackee and salt fish and festivals sat cold until Dad ate them. I watched them disappear.

The eye kept me awake. It was the wait. Silence, like a threat, pressed up against my throat. The rain stopped. No wind. I looked through the boarded window onto the street. People were standing outside their house, looking, hands akimbo. Someone, a woman crying, sat on the sidewalk. Brown dogs from both next doors sniffed the trees that use to be in their backyards.

I waited. The eye moved over us, the quiet hub of the hurricane.

The rain and wind whipped up again. I was relieved that the wait was over and that the worst would now come and go.

I sat through hours of the second half in the dry tub. The door was latched to keep it from flying open. Inside, I heard the outside rip and roar and howl. The rain's sound was a city of dragging feet scraping across asphalt and concrete. Against the zinc roofs, it was the steady streaming sound of fish frying.

When I came out, they were hunched around the kerosene lamp at the kitchen table. Mum or dad had cooked the meats in the refrigerator to keep them from going bad. The food filled the table. They ate. My sister picked off a piece of ham with her hands, ate it and took another. My mother watched and said nothing. The wind shook the back door. My father cracked the bones of the chicken leg in his mouth. He sucked the marrow, slurping. The rain beat against the shut aluminum windows.

I went to bed with no words and no food. Overnight the rain softened and the wind wound down, but I tossed and twisted in my sheets till morning. There was nothing to calm me. My heart hammered all night.

The next day we checked for damage. The scale read 84 pounds. The living room was flooded. Pieces of our zinc roof were in the yard across the street. My heart wouldn't stop pounding. Our dogs had shat and vomited all over the verandah. And fat flies feasted on the mess. My mother was crying over the kitchen sink. The island had lost all power and phone service. We were cut off from the world. My father sat with his back to her, still eating the meats cooked the night before. His hand wouldn't stop moving from the food to his mouth. A fly circled the cured and cooked flesh. The voice from the battery-run radio announced, "This was the worst natural disaster in Jamaica's history, half a million without homes, 26 dead, damage in the millions, no light, no power…, back on the Atlantic…, strengthening…."

"At first it was a tempest, off the coast of Africa. Then it was a storm off the coast of the Lesser Antilles. Then it was the most intense hurricane to ever travel the Atlantic, beating all records" for its feeding off the warm ocean currents. "The lowest barometric pressure in the history of hurricane record-keeping." For days the news fed us its story.

At first I was worried that I would fail. It started as a dream that I was naked and paralyzed in the street. It started as a dream that I was falling and falling and flailing. There was no ground to catch me. Then it was a summer of summer classes all day and tutoring into the night. Then I was thinner and someone said I looked good. Then I was straight A's. Then I looked A okay. And then I remembered to miss meals to stay on top. And then, and then, and then, I no longer dreamt I was falling. And then I was in the eye of it. I was feeding off an ocean of anxiety.

My heart hammered.

My aunt from Brooklyn visited us the summer before the storm. We picked her up from the airport. She hadn't seen me in years. When she hugged me, her hands ran down my back. Then they spanned my waist.

"You're too thin," she told me.

Her hands moved to my hips. Her thumbs pressed against the points of my pelvis, against the slipping waistline of my jeans.

"You don't look well." She stared into my face.

Her grip held me in place. I didn't know what to say. She looked at mom and dad standing beside me and their eyes looked pleading. She brought a piece of newspaper out of her purse and pressed it into my palm.

"There was a woman who died. Make sure you read this."

It was an obituary. A singer. A white woman in America with eyes as big and a face as stretched as mine. At first she collapsed on stage while singing, "Top of the World". Then they thought she was getting well. And then one day they found her naked and dead to the world on the floor of her walk-in closet. Worlds away from me. Her heart failed.

When Gilbert hit, I weighed 20 pounds less than the singer who died. My heart kept hammering. I couldn't stop.

It was just a tempest, till it traveled the sea. It was just a storm off the Lesser Antilles. Then it fattened in the ocean. Then it was a hurricane shedding water and eating trees and eating roofs and eating lives. And then it was much-needed rain in the Midwest of the US. And there it died, starved for water.

My father believed in the ocean. It would clean you. It could cure you. When I had a cold, we went to the beach.

"The ocean will fix you up," he told me. Then he held my hand and walked me into the waves. It was warm. It was alive against my skin.

"Go under. Don't be afraid," he told me. Then he pressed my head till it sank into the sea. It was cold, then warm, in my hair. It rushed and roared into my ears. I gave in to it. I curved into a ball and grabbed my knees. I was a ball, bobbing, buoyant. I floated free.

When I came up for air, he smiled. "Good."

"I'm better," I smiled back. I felt the snot running out the channels of my nose.

He smiled again, "Good."

I smiled back and let the snot drain down my chin into the sea. I watched it thin out and disappear.

Gilbert left. I was down to 82 pounds.

My heart hammered all night. I dreamt till daylight. I dreamt the singer who died was in my yearbook and no one knew who she was and no one noticed her but me. She was flat and dull against the page and all I knew about her was her thin smile in the black and white picture of her face. But I knew her in another way. In another way I knew her face. I dreamt that I tried to ask who she was, but no words would come out of my mouth. I tried to ask with my eyes, but they kept smiling and everyone kept smiling back even though I heard them whispering, "something's wrong…"

In the morning, my mother woke me up with my bathing suit in her hand. "We're going to the beach."

I'd never seen the shore so clean and the sky so clear.

"Good washing, I give Gilbert that, at least," my father said. He took my hand. We walked me into the waves. It was cold and choppy. It pushed against us.

"Just keep going," he pulled me along. At that moment I was a little girl, falling behind, trying to keep up, not wanting to complain that this is too hard and that I want to be carried just for now, please. The water splashed into my eyes and my nose. I coughed and spat.

"You can make it," his grip tightened. And I pushed ahead against the tide, deeper into the sea. We stopped and a wave swelled a few feet away, crested high, then swallowed us. A swirling. A switch of worlds. From sunshine to dark. Blues blinding and choking and snatching and pressing and lifting and taking over. When it crashed, I spat and gulped for air. Dad kept his hold.

My heart hammered against the surge and I felt myself spinning and slipping. Something was wrong. I opened my eyes and Dad was Oceanus commanding the waves. I blinked and he was my father again. He towered over me, his grip, tight. An inescapable lifeguard. The wet hair on his chest sat in swirls of gray and black, curly and glistening. He was bald and his belly stuck out, but his brown eyes looked as young as mine. For a minute, I saw us both bald, standing deep in the crashing waves, looking like pieces of each other.

A wave of nausea overwhelmed me and I vomited bile. It was white and sour and sticky and salty. Dad let go of my hand and stepped back. We both watched as it trailed from my chin into the sea, thinned in the water and disappeared.

He asked if I was better.

I shook my head and wiped my lips with the back of my hand.

"I want to go home."

Talk of the Town was the only local bakery, but for days after the hurricane, it was closed. For days after the hurricane, I would walk the length of the street, slowly, taking in the bright skies which spread without stopping, which spread without being broken by a single tree, which spread like a still sea of blue without its floating rafts of white. And when I got to Talk of the Town, I would press my face against the glass doors, look past the red and white "Closed" sign and watch the empty shelves. We waited for bread, like we waited for clean water, like we waited for the power to return.

In the meantime, my mother made festivals. She mixed the cornmeal she'd bought for the dogs with a little sugar and a little water and a pinch of salt, a pinch of baking powder and a pat of butter. She stood silent over the kitchen counter and kneaded it, pushing and pulling the dough over and over again.   Shaping and reshaping it until it was enough. She made festivals for breakfast, for lunch and for dinner. She served festivals with fish, festivals with chicken, festivals with any meat we had. It became our rice and our bread when we found ourselves with no rice and no bread and just the cornmeal meant for the dogs.

She worked in her housedress, the one crowded with faded flowers, and seemed anchored to the stove.

Each morning I'd wake up to the sound of her in the kitchen. The loud hiss of hot oil attacking raw dough. The shuffle of worn-out bed slippers sliding across tile flooring and, briefly, the *ting-tin* of her teaspoon hitting the sides of her coffee mug. And the sipping slurp that came after it.

Every morning I'd wake up and take inventory of my bones. Collarbones. Ribs. Stomach cove. Hipbones.

Shallow breaths.

Hummingbird heart.

Every morning I rubbed my pelvic bones like worry stones and lingered a little in bed.

School was still out. No one came to get me up.

When I would finally make it into the dining room and try to walk past the kitchen, I'd watch for her looking. And sometimes she would throw me a look: "Eat." Or sometimes she would offer me a plate: "Eat." Or sometimes she would look away and turn to the stove and turn the festivals so that they wouldn't burn: "Eat."

We were trying to recover. And my dad took me fishing for doctor fish.

It was a month after the storm. All the trees were cleared from the streets and the broken branches were being cut down. We had some power, but school was still out. Some things were like they were before, but some things were still broken. We had some power back and the news carried stories about too much time out of school, what's going to happen when exams roll around, it's better to get them back as soon as possible; it's better to get them back to normal. We had our roof back and my mom went back to following me around the house asking what's wrong and why you don't eat and why you making us sick with worry and what's going to happen if you don't just eat something? And my dad sometimes listened and watched and sighed and said, "Everybody have them cross to bear." And Mom would run her veined hands over her face and hunch her shoulders. And then I was heavier than I've ever been; the heaviest cross she ever had to bear.

She had a red bathing suit that she wore the summer she was 16, the same summer Jamaica got its independence. She was thin then. And, lucky for me, she keeps everything. It was still in the plastic bag it came in with mothballs to guard it. And, lucky for me, everything old is new again. It had a simple hourglass cut and the legs and crotch were the same length. It banded around my torso, butt and hips.

We were in Jamaica and, lucky for me, we saw a lot of old matinees with American movie stars like Marilyn Monroe, Greta Garbo, Grace Kelly and Ingrid Bergman and they wore bathing suits like the one my mom wore when she was sixteen and that I then wore when I was sixteen and she was 42. And it was fashionable again. And, lucky for me, it fit—again. And, lucky for us, we were in Jamaica and we had a TV station and cinemas and we got to see stars like Madonna, who was like a virgin over and over again, and Michael J. Fox, who was zooming back and forth to the future in the revamped carcass of a DeLorean. And, lucky for us, everything old was new again and time was as fluid and endless as the sea and though everything sometimes changed, it would all remain the same.

"We're going to the beach." Dad was in his trunks; Mom, her housedress. I had just come home from church with the wafer and wine still staining my tongue. I sat on my bed, savoring the Holy Communion and the loose way my Easter dress draped over me and the loose way the altar boys looked at me and the loose way the altar girl vestments had swam around me and the loose way feeling like a good girl made me feel. They came to the door and stood like guards watching over me and stood like a wall blocking me in. Dad had on his swimming trunks. Mom handed me hers, the one she wore when she was my age, when Jamaica finally got its independence, when change seemed poised to sweep over the island and her. It was still folded in the plastic package it came it. It was as good as new.

When we went to the beach that Easter Sunday, the sky and the water were the clearest and calmest I'd seen them since Gilbert. I thought he would make me go in. But he told me to do whatever I wanted. A couple of Rastafarians were standing beside an old wooden fishing boat. They were dark and glistening with sand and salt. Their hair fell in thick brown and black locks down their backs and over their shoulders. As soon as they saw dad, they smiled and shouted, "Hail up, bredren!" They seemed like old friends. My Dad hugged them both. Smiles shone everywhere. Then they pushed the boat out into the waves. When they were in and rowing away, dad shouted back to me: "We going fishing for some doctorfish! Relax till we get back!"

Recovery was hard. Recovering is hard.

Gilbert was gone and I was still 16. The school year was almost over. It was almost summer again and some of the trees had grown back and some of the grass had grown back and some of the roofs had been put back and almost all of the power was back.

I was better, but I wasn't better. I wore Dad's suit jacket, the one he wore when he worked for the power company. I wore it all the time, even over my school uniform and even after Sister St. Vincent called me *Suzy-Q* from across the cafeteria and told me to take that jacket off because this is the tropics and it is not cold, it is never cold and I have no need for it and no business wearing it. I kept it on even after I stood in the bathroom stall and heard the whispers about all the girls who got pregnant during the month after Gilbert when the power was out and we were stuck in the dark with hardly a thing to do to keep from going mad except throw some caution to the wind, like them girls who now pregnant and I bet you that girl with the jacket, you know the one getting fatter and fatter, I bet any money, she one of them, for sure. I wore the jacket all the time and it kept some of the chill off. Even so, my fingernails were blue and I shivered in the sunshine.

On the first day of summer vacation, I went to the beach. I wore my own bathing suit and my father's old suit jacket, the one he wore when he worked for the power company. It kept some of the chill off as I walked along the paved road that ran for three miles from our house to the nearest beach. And when I got there, I tilted my head towards the sun: I wanted to be washed in warmth. I listened and watched as the waves washed in and over the sand and in and over each other, rolling and unfurling and curling and tumbling back.

I breathed deeply and pulled a sigh from the well inside me. I sent it out with a gust of air. I felt time flow before me and around me, rolling and unfurling, curling and tumbling back.

Lina and Baby

Amy Olassa

On a Saturday evening at a 5-for-Rupees 500.00 beauty salon, Lina is getting her eyebrows threaded. Her eyes water and her fingers hold the skin taut while the beautician unspools and twists the thread expertly, and rakes the skin between Lina's eyebrows. In the next chair, Baby lowers a worn copy of a magazine, turns to Lina and says, "Did I tell you, Joji's stalker might have killed herself."

Lina shoots Baby a look from the corner of her eye, but the beautician doesn't bat an eyelid. She carries on threading Lina's left eyebrow at a blistering pace, pressing Lina back into the chair. Beauticians must hear all kinds of gossip, but also, the beautician doesn't know that Joji is Baby's boyfriend. Baby is reading her magazine again, but her forehead is in folds and her mouth is in a pout.

After the beautician moves to another client, unspooling more thread, Lina looks over at Baby. "Joji has a stalker?" she asks.

Baby closes the magazine, drops it on her lap and flips and flops her right hand. "Well," she says. "There's this girl who likes him, and she threatens suicide if he doesn't call her constantly and text her and things like that."

"Things like that," Lina repeats, unsettled at this revelation.

Baby is beautiful. Like a slab of soft butter, a jar of clear ghee. Her complexion is neither fair nor dusky; her features are full and fresh, she has lovely, thick eyebrows and her hair is black silk. She's the sort of beauty no one would associate with competition in love or heartbreak, regular-people disappointments.

"And how did you find out that she might have, you know, killed herself?" Lina asks, her voice low.

Baby sighs. "Don't you listen to anything I say? Joji talks to her every week and this week he didn't call because he and I had a fight about her, and she texted and threatened to do something, and now she won't answer his calls and she always answers his calls!"

Lina is reluctant to probe further but can't help but ask why Joji is close with this girl who's clearly vulnerable, and why this doesn't bother Baby. Why has it gone so far? Lina thinks Baby and Joji's romance is careless and erratic, but she worries her own ideas about love are too conventional. Even as a teenager her notions about infatuation were more serious. Like in real, grown-up relationships, with rough patches and ups and downs, and at the end, it would all be fine because of an absolute commitment to keep going, because there was no way out. This was before Rohan, when Lina was young and naïve and now she's glad for solitude and friends, the apartment she shares with Baby, even her nerve-wracking job as a Junior Account Manager at ILICI bank. She values all of this believing contentment is temporary; the natural state of adulthood is duty-bound and joyless.

Baby seems to notice Lina's discomfort. She puts a hand on Lina's arm. "Oh, it's not like that, Lina," she says, her voice sweet and soothing.

"You know Joji loves me. This girl, she's an only child and she has no friends. Joji loves me and she knows that, but she's a little too attached and she's very lonely," Baby says.

Lina tries to smile. Baby is so certain of herself, even in situations that could break her.

The girl sitting on the other side of Baby doesn't try to hide that she was listening to their conversation. The girl smiles at Lina and Baby. "Hi," she says and waves at them. The girl is having her hair colored and her legs waxed at the same time. Salon workers crowd around her, two work on her hair and two on her legs. She must be a regular at the salon and a generous tipper. When she arrived, the salon workers greeted her like they would a friend. They discussed husbands and boyfriends, and ribbed each other about their sex lives. The girl is dressed in the same beauty parlor sarong as Lina and Baby – clingy, synthetic fabric, tied at their chests and ending at their calves, and Lina notices the love bites on the girls neck, down to her shoulders, one underneath her bottom lip. In a couple of days it will lighten then disappear, but for now it is what it is. The girl touches her face and neck. "My boyfriend likes to make these marks." She giggles. "He's such a child, he doesn't like to share." Lina and Baby smile at the girl.

"Her boyfriend is an idiot," Baby whispers in Lina's ear. They made eyes at the girl and chuckle into cupped palms, but Lina is thinking about Rohan, how he had often marked her neck the same way.

Lina identifies Elmon Joseph as soon as she enters the Coffee Break Café. He's wearing the blue and black-checkered shirt he said he would be wearing, and she is dressed in a pastel-pink salwar kameez to help him identify her. He's at a table by a large window that overlooks Brigade Road, and she knows Elmon has seen her because he's looking at her. He pushes back the wicker chair, stands up and leans over the granite table, his hands grasping the edge of the table. *Hi, hello*, they say and he gestures to the chair across from him and she sits down carefully, conscious of her every movement. Lina quickly notes the pressed, formal pants, the gold watch on his wrist, and his thick, well-groomed mustache, all of which reminds her of her father. She wipes the sweat that collects above her upper lip, fans herself and looks around the room as if she's wondering if the air conditioner is broken.

"It's very hot," he says, leaning forward and she smiles and nods affirmatively, and she thinks she'd like to leave.

Elmon Joseph is twenty-eight years old and works as a Project Manager with a tech company. These are the only details Lina knows about Elmon, and even as she arrived at the café, she was certain she didn't want to marry a man named Elmon, that Lina Elmon doesn't sound right, that anyone whose parents thought it was a good idea to name their son Elmon might expect their future grandchildren to have ridiculous names.

The waiter brings coffee and a plate of cookies that are delicious, but the conversation is bumpy and unsatisfactory. *How are you? What do you do? How long have you worked there? Do you like Bangalore? Do you prefer coffee or tea? Cats or dogs?*

As soon as her parents found out that she and Rohan were broken up, they wanted to find Lina a match. It was not just her parents, even Baby tried to set her up. Because—*why are you alone?* Suddenly, at twenty-four, being single is an anomaly and no one understands her fatigue; love is too big an investment of time, potential and energy, only to lose everything in a flash or burn down with it.

Lina distracts herself with the busy traffic outside, the assortment of stalls that line the street and the crowd of pedestrians walking by. She doesn't want to compare Elmon to Rohan who she now remembers as lively and young, in every way the opposite of Elmon. An hour goes by and they leave the Café, Lina politely agreeing to meet Elmon again but wanting to never return, to just keep walking and maybe she'll end up in someone else's life. Later, when Baby asks about Elmon, Lina can remember only one thing they spoke about. Elmon's fathers name begins with an L and his mother's name is Elsa, and so the *El* attached to *Mon*, that in Malayalam means *son* was how Elmon got his name. Baby shakes her head, her eyebrows raised. "Lina, this is not good. How can you not remember anything else?" she says.

Then she asks, "You didn't find him attractive at all?"

"He looks older," Lina says. "I'm not trying to be cruel, he's evaluating me too and maybe if we met in different circumstances, I would have noticed qualities to admire."

"Then why are you meeting him again?" Baby asks.

"Because *I found him unattractive* is not a good enough reason to say no."

"It's good enough for men to turn down women," says Baby.

"We're not men," Lina replies.

Lina is sitting with Baby on the balcony of their Cooke Town apartment, drinking tea and watching the busy intersection. Baby shakes her head. "I just don't understand Joji," she says. "Why is this even happening, why must I worry about strange women obsessed with my boyfriend?"

It turns out that Joji's stalker is alive and well. She spent the weekend with her mother. They went shopping and she simply didn't bother to answer Joji's calls. Lina is relieved the girl is safe but the whole situation seems twisted. Baby refuses to tell Joji to stop, she will not admit this bothers her. "Why should I ask him to stop talking to people, I have my dignity and pride. I'm better than that," she says with a hand to her chest.

Baby's restraint surprises Lina. She would have handled things differently. She and Rohan had been possessive of one other and their endless fights about this girl and that boy had made her feel petty and small. To act with such self-control feels impossible to Lina.

In the evening, Joji comes over holding red roses, a box of pastries from *Sugar* and mutton biryani from *Rahman's,* and he promises that he's done talking to the girl, it's not like they know each other anyway and he's told the girl to talk to her parents, or a friend, or a person she can trust and find the right kind of support, because he can't help her anymore, it's beyond his capabilities, he's done. Baby is pacified, for now.

They eat dinner and watch *Dance Stars* and Lina tries to focus on the television show while Baby and Joji canoodle on the divan. They are clingier and more emotional than usual. In one week Joji will move to London for a work assignment, and he's excitedly making plans for a final trip that weekend, to Nandi Hills. Lina is always included in every plan, as all all their friends, and she thinks how she and Rohan had been the opposite, always alone at the movies and ice cream shops and on long walks. At first it had been exciting, just them, they needed no one else, but it turned out to be a sort of deprivation. They ran out of things to talk about because they were always together, just the two of them. They quickly found out how little they had in common and one day, like ice melting to water, they stopped talking altogether.

Lina is uncomfortable with Baby and Joji's PDA and simultaneously left in wonderment. They've been together a decade and Joji's always showering Baby with gifts and attention. Baby's real name is Annie and Joji's real name is George, but everyone who knows them as a couple knows them by their nicknames. When she sees them together Lina's certain that any number of women couldn't distract Joji's affection for Baby, and maybe her heartbreak with Rohan was a single round of bad luck and the next time she meets Elmon, or another man her parents want her to meet, she should let something happen. Baby once confided in Lina that she and Joji haven't yet had sex. "We do everything but not *that*," she said, though Lina didn't think that was such a big deal. She and Rohan had done it, but she did not tell this to Baby.

Lina works at ILICI Bank's corporate office on M.G Road, managing credit accounts for mid-size corporations. She works six days a week and spends the seventh day worrying about the next workweek. The pay is not worth the stress of managing large numbers, the constant terror of a misplaced decimal point, an amount recorded and transacted in error. Baby is the Assistant Manager at the adjoining ILICI branch office. She tends to clients all day, getting wrung out by her Manager and clients in turn, but she's a seasoned employee and has learnt how to handle the turbulence. What really eases Baby's workdays is Ram, processor of checks and demand drafts, Baby's "work husband" Joji likes to tease.

At breakfast, in the office cafeteria, Lina orders Pongal, and Baby and Ram get the Idli-Vada combo plate. This is Ram's favorite food and Baby likes to think they have this in common. Ram is fairly good-looking and always well dressed but lacks personality, and Lina cannot understand why Baby is so taken with Ram. As usual, they are bickering. Baby wants Ram to join them on the Nandi Hills trip. "What'll I do on a hill," Ram says. He spoons up the last of his sambhar and won't look at Baby.

"You do nothing. It's beautiful and peaceful and that's why we're going," she says.

"I'm busy this weekend," he says, though just a minute ago he said he had no plans. Ram stands up, gathers his plate, glass and spoon, and Baby has her head down and she stares at her plate.

"I don't care," Baby insists after Ram leaves.

Unlike Joji, Ram is aloof and moody. He's one of those people you cannot really depend on – he forgets to meet Baby after they make plans, cancels on her when he feels like it, and places his convenience ahead of everything and everyone else.

This – Baby and Ram – is not unusual. All around the cafeteria, and downstairs in the lobby and in conference rooms, Lina observes employees in pairs.

The drive to Nandi Hills through the morning fog and the winding road on the hillside is magical and dangerous. Baby and Joji are arguing again, about him moving to London. "Baby, Baby," Joji pleads and Baby is unmoved. Her face is stone, and from the backseat Lina notices that even when the car drops into potholes, Baby's the only one who isn't thrown around. When they get to the top of the hill, Lina detaches from the couple and makes small talk with the others in their troop, and as she walks back from Suicide Point where people linger to discuss the jilted, heartbroken lovers who leapt off the cliff, Lina's cellphone begins to buzz with a string of text messages from Rohan who wants to know how she's doing.

During inventory week, Lina accompanies the Senior Account Manager, Dipti, on tours of client factory units located beyond city limits where the fields are endless, as are the roads, and the mountains are green, and the landscape is marked with clusters of dusty villages and industrial buildings, flocks of goats and pairs of cows grazing on green grass. The bank pays for A.C taxis, the clients cover the meals, and it almost feels like an annual school picnic. Almost. Lina is unnerved at Dipti's haphazard method of verifying collateral. Dipti picks items at random and verifies only those. The Senior Account Manager is focused and adept in her conversations with the unit personnel. They discuss operations and forecasts for the coming quarters. They walk through warehouses and stores with inventory lists that are endless.

"What about the rest? Shouldn't we check everything?" Lina asks. She worries, how can they be certain the items listed are actually stacked in the stores, and the machinery with the given specifications are as numbered, how can they know these assets are as valued on paper and aren't promised as collateral to another bank, how can a proper verification be accomplished in under five hours?

"Don't be silly," Dipti scolds, a stern mentor. "They don't actually expect us to count every item, then we'll need a week at each facility. This is routine and we have a mutual understanding with our clients. Trust, faith, you know, and there are ways to retrieve a loss. Insurance for one."

Despite these assurances, Lina is nervous and wrung out by the end of the week. She wants to be done with the bank.

"Oh, Lina," Baby sighs when Lina tells her. "Just ask yourself, do you want your boss's job in five years? Or your boss's boss's job in, like, ten? If not, you have your answer."

It's good advice. Think about the future. Whatever it is today, compound it and ask yourself if you still want it.

"Nothing is worth being this miserable," Baby says. She's sprawled out on the divan, leaning on Ram while he reads the newspaper and Lina does not want to discuss the matter further with Ram around, and now that Joji's gone, he's always around. She wants to tell Baby that Ram is bad news, but people only hear what they want to hear. Often, Lina finds Baby just staring into space, a vacant look in her eyes, and she worries that Baby is depressed.

At first, after Joji left, Baby cried every day. She cried herself to sleep and cried when she woke up, she cried over Joji's favorite foods and even over blue nail polish, Joji's favorite color. When she ran out of tears, she became angry with him for going away. "I cannot believe him," she said. "He says he's doing it for us, but he didn't bother to ask me what I want!"

"Baby, why didn't you just tell him not to go?" Lina asked.

"We've been together eleven years, Lina. Eleven years! Do I have to tell him?" Baby snapped. She had a point, but Lina also understood Joji's intentions. They're getting older and Joji wants to settle down. He wants to marry Baby and he's thinking ahead. He's thinking that a job in the U.K is promising and better money, and you don't stay because you're content where you are and you're scared to do the next thing.

That night Lina updates her resume. She calls and emails friends and puts out the word that she's seeking other job opportunities. "Not a bank, anything else," she tells them.

On the weekend, Lina boards the last sleeper bus at K.R Market and arrives at her parents' home in time for breakfast. She avoids visits as her parents have become intensely focused on her marriage prospects. Her parents have been married twenty-six years, unhappy for as long as she can remember. They barely talk, which is an improvement, before which, their many fights, on the streets of their town, in the car, and once at a wedding with over a thousand guests as witnesses provided enough material for small-town gossip. Lina attempted to sidestep all of this by finding love on her own, disqualifying herself from the rigors of an arranged match, which would only reignite gossip about her parents. Though her parents loathe each other, they maintain a strong attachment to Lina. "Your visits liven up the house," her mother says. "Your father smiles."

Lina's mother talks about Elmon like he's already her son-in-law. She insists that Lina must speak with Elmon's mother on the phone. "It'll make a good impression that you're home for the weekend. They'll know you'll make a good daughter-in-law," she says.

Lina tells her parents she's meeting an old schoolmate and goes to Rohan's house. They've been texting, but this time it's different. This time there are no promises, no obligations, at least this is what Rohan wants and Lina has decided she will not ask for more.

His parents are away for the weekend and she's been in his house a hundred times before, on the couch in the living room and on the bed in his room. Lina's sitting on a chair at his study desk, and comforted by the familiarity of the space and his company, she mentions Elmon, in a casual manner, because there's still a compulsion to share every truth. Rohan is quiet. His eyes latch on to hers and when they kiss, he bites her lips raw and his hands feel strong, forceful. Before, she couldn't respect his hesitation to commit, that he kept her hidden from his parents and his brother, and now, when they can be in the moment and move on he seems to want something else. As he puts his hands on her waist, his face in her neck Lina thinks they're a puzzle she cannot decipher, opaque like muddy water.

On the eve of her 26th birthday, Baby breaks up with Joji. There's cake and flowers and beautifully wrapped packages in the living room — gifts from Joji dropped off by delivery services that ring their doorbell through the day. Baby becomes distraught when she sees these things, so Lina gives the cake to the maid, hides the gifts and dumps the flowers in the trashcan in the street. Joji calls Lina a million times, pleading with her to reason with Baby, but there's nothing to be done. Baby's already grieving. She's withdrawn to her room. She will not tell Lina why she ended things with Joji, and Lina can only ask so many times.

One evening, Baby's crying in her room, and Lina sits on Baby's bed, holding her hand. Baby's lost weight. Her hair isn't combed and her eyes are sunken. "It'll be okay," Lina says. "It's not the end of the world. I'm single and I'm fine."

"You're not single, you're seeking. And what about Elmon?" Baby asks and Lina shudders.

"What about him?" she says. Her second date with Elmon wasn't any better than the first. She barely spoke and she was nauseous.

Baby sits up, looks at Lina and says, "I slept with Ram." She's gazing at Lina's face, waiting for a reaction.

"Okay," Lina says, carefully. They share an apartment and work at the same bank, but they both have secrets. Lina stopped responding to Rohan's text messages that became sexual and intense in a way that didn't include her, but ambushed her.

"We're sort of together," Baby says and bites her lip. It's none of Lina's business, but it looks like Baby desperately wants to tell her more and Baby wants her opinion.

"Since when?" Lina asks but Baby says she can't tell her.

"What do you mean by sort of together?" Linda asks.

"We had sex, after Joji left," Baby replies.

"So you and Joji are really over?" Lina asks.

Baby bites her lips and hesitates. "Yes," she says, but as if it's a question and Lina reads guilt and sorrow and anguish on Baby's face.

"But Joji is good to you. Apart from that situation with the girl, which I must say worried me deeply," says Lina.

"But my whole life is here, Lina," Baby says. "I cannot give it up just like that and move to London and start all over again, just for him." And Baby presses her pillow to her mouth and tears flow down her cheeks, and her eyes are swollen and red. "I'm good at my job and I love it here!" she cries.

"I understand," Lina says to Baby, but she really wants to tell Baby that Baby doesn't have to be with Ram just because she's not with Joji, it will be good to be on her own for a while, at least until the clouds clear. But she doesn't. She leans in and holds Baby.

"Don't cry," Lina says.

Lina's transition to Progress Intel feels quick, like daybreak after a dark, moonless night. She finds that Progress Intel is everything ILICI Bank was not. The culture is informal. Deliverables are collaborative. Workdays are long, but manageable. The same week Lina leaves ILICI

Bank and joins Progress Intel, Ram moves into their apartment. He arrives with two suitcases, walks past Lina into Baby's bedroom and shuts the door.

"Just a few of his things," says Baby.

"He won't be here all the time," Baby assures Lina, but Ram is over all the time. And when he's around, the mood is pensive and charged. Lina feels like she's always walking in on a fight. Baby's nervous and silly, unreadable, secretive and fiercely protective of Ram. The whole thing feels vague and slippery.

On Lina's third date with Elmon, after a three-course meal at a five-star restaurant that he insists on paying for, and perhaps emboldened by the two orders of scotch in his belly, Elmon asks Lina if she has been in love, and then, if she's ever been touched. She's eating her dessert when he says this. She carefully places the spoon on the table, studies her plate and taps the tabletop with a finger. He's watching her, undaunted, unashamed of his encroachment, and she's surprised at herself, that she has permitted him the liberty. She wonders about the influences that inserted such a curiosity in his mind, how he could think it was acceptable to ask her such a question.

"You know how it is over here, in the city. Life is fast and it's possible, to get carried away," he explains.

If she says no, that she's never been involved with anyone, he'll probably say, *I'm happy to marry you Lina, lets take this forward.* And if she says yes, she's been with other people, then he'll say, *I'm sorry Lina that I'm still sitting at this table with you, and no, this will not work out*, and she will be released. She's heard of such inappropriate enquiries, always to a friend of a friend, or the friend of a cousin. No one will admit it happened to them. Her heartbeat is louder and her hands tremble, and she's tempted to say, *I've been more than just touched* and that will put an end to Elmon and her, but this is private information she will never share with this man. She's angry that she feels compelled to respond, yet she shakes her head, and having received the answer he desires, Elmon smiles. As she watches him flag down a waiter for the check, the knot in her throat feels heavier, sharper, and she wonders how much longer she must carry on this façade.

At the salon, Lina gets a mani-pedi and Baby cuts her hair short, cropped close to her scalp, a helmet of sharp bristles. "I wanted a new look," Baby says and runs a hand over her hair. Lina stares at Baby's reflection in the mirror. The salon hair stylist, Usha, stands next to Lina and bites her bottom lip, holds the scissors up and away from her.

"Thank you, Usha," Baby says. She stands up and long strands of hair drop off her shoulder. Baby removes the salon cape and drapes it on the chair. Usha puts the scissors away, fetches the broom and begins to sweep the floor, and she looks at Baby constantly.

"Baby, you always look good," Lina says.

Baby runs her hand over her head, again and again. "Oh, my head feels so light. I feel so free!" she says.

Lina has noticed that lately Ram isn't around much. When she asks Baby about Ram, Baby pulls out her wallet busying herself. "He's doing great," she says. "His mother is looking for a bride for him, he wants to get married this year."

Lina cocks her head. "What did you say?" she asks. "What about the two of you?"

Baby turns to Lina and grins, showing all her teeth, her eyes wide and open and says, "Yeah, that's how it is." She shrugs.

"But what about you?" Lina asks again.

"Oh, I don't know!" says Baby. "We're together, we're not together, we're together, we're not together." She chuckles and her eyes tear up, and Lina notices the dark circles that frame Baby's eyes, the acne that marks her butter-like skin, the light rash on her forehead.

"Men are so irrational," Baby says, after a moment.

"So are women," Lina says. "But Baby, we're talking about Ram, specifically about Ram."

Baby sighs and leans back on the counter packed with scissors and combs, and hairbrushes, hair dryers and hair products. "Ram hates Joji," Baby sighs.

Lina shakes her head. "But you were with Joji and then Ram came along. And Baby, I should have said this sooner, but Ram's awful. To you, to everyone, and now he's looking to marry someone else?"

Baby grabs Lina's arm. "He had a difficult childhood, Lina! He doesn't get along with his parents, he was in a boarding school all his life, he doesn't know how to love!" Baby says.

"He doesn't know how to love?" Lina asks and Baby winces. Lina wants to say more things but she doesn't want to hurt Baby. She sits back in her chair, folds her arms around her body and watches Baby, who throws her head back and stares at the ceiling, tears streaming down the sides of her face. Lina remembers an evening at Rohan's home when his brother returned unexpectedly and Rohan hid her in a storage room at the back of his house, pressed a key to the front door into her hand and instructed her to let herself out later, when he took his brother out. She waited there for an hour, among piles of old newspapers and old cans and barrels, her heart pounding that she would be found in that room, like a thief, or worse, a woman with broken morals, and later, when the fear wore off she felt mortified that he had hidden her away, abandoned her so quickly.

Lina said *no* to Elmon, but already, she has another date with another possible match. There will be another, then another. They will speak about the weather, if they like dogs or cats, if they're religious or not, and they will try and fail to gauge other, more critical things —

money habits and other habits, how they value relationships, if they've been loved, if they know how to love and be loved. It's possible that one of these conversations with one of these men will be better than the rest. It will be more honest and pleasant, they might even have something in common, and Lina will tell this man that she's in no rush. They must take the time they need; it is the beginning of uncertainty.

Betty Davis Eyes

Hannah Eko

Tanisha is saying that finding Betty Davis is *our sacred duty*.

She always speaks like that, like she's gunning for lead in drama class.

I watch her foot as she digs the toe of her red Converse into the sidewalk. Back and forth so that the top makes a scrunch sound. The wind slaps my chest and I zip my hoody tighter.

Digging toe into ground is Tanisha body language for I'm About To Make A Very Bad Decision.

I met her in AP Psychology last semester. We were both in the back row and I let her cheat off my unit tests. She ended up getting an A in the class and I got a B+.

"You're not going to bitch out on me?" she asks, eyes witching.

She asks this as if we hadn't just taken two buses to get to this exact quiet street, lonely with trees.

Tanisha is jutting shoulders and hollow face, a brown-skinned wanna-be punk girl with fried green hair. It's hard to imagine much energy is contained in something so skinny, but Tanisha is a walking sun.

I nod at her wide forehead and for the sixty billionth time, think about how I will kill myself tomorrow.

"I don't think this a good idea," I finally answer.

I'll probably use Darnell's leftover pills. Google says it's less messy that way.

I'm not sad about it or anything.

When I finally decided to do it, whatever was squeezing my heart in like old trash stopped its pull.

Even my mom says I've been in a better mood this past week.

It's the magic point between sunset and setting and the sky is a bluesy purple, the street is all wet with hours ago rain. I finger a rusty nail in an electric post and let Tanisha go on about Betty Davis and *ordained journeys* and *black girl magic*.

There's no real use arguing with Tanisha's logic.

It'd be like talking to the radio.

"You're really gonna stop me from meeting The Queen of Funk?" she asks, "You know this is my dream."

Tanisha does not talk about how this dream began about fifty minutes ago after we both finished watching the Betty Davis documentary at Regent Theater.

Tanisha does not mention how I was the one who caught the throwaway shot of Nancy B's Bakery, which helped us zero in on the fact that Betty Davis must've lived on West Seventh.

She also doesn't talk about how Betty Davis does not want to be found.

I mean, even her old band can't find her.

Tanisha whoops her arms up and down like a crazy propeller, ready to move.

"What's wrong with you?" she asks, "Her voice was like the sweetest lullaby."

"Sure," I say even though Betty Davis did not sound like something you'd sing a baby, "But that doesn't mean she's gonna be happy about two random stalkers showing up at her door."

Tanisha sighs, pushes her foot into the ground like she wants to leave a dent.

And then starts walk-running towards West Seventh.

I've always followed people like Tanisha, people who I think will light me up.

And then I just end up in the audience alone, clapping.

Before Tanisha, it was Ashima, an Indian girl with a supermodel complex and me as photographer.

After tomorrow I won't even be here, so why bother switching up.

So, even though I'm about four inches shorter than Tanisha, I do my best to keep up with her long strides.

"I wonder what she's going to tell me," Tanisha says slowing down.

"Maybe she hates fans," I say.

"Sunny. She wants us to find her, it's all over the film," Tanisha says, "You've got to increase your scope of imagination."

I'm supposed to agree, but I look at the ground.

I know her big eyes are searching my face for an affirmative.

My silence balloons around me until it's so big it pops.

"You're so annoying," Tanisha says and starts walking fast again.

She keeps checking her phone and murmuring under her breath, curls of vapor escaping like cigarette smoke.

It's just us in this street.

Dewy cars, naked trees with gnarled branches lifting to the sky. A forgotten toy car turned over on its side. It's like we're the only people alive.

Seven years from now, Tanisha will get exactly what she wants. She'll glue 686 maxi pads smeared with red glitter onto the house of a right-wing mayor.

Her hair will be blue.

She will become famous.

Tonight, she doesn't know that.

Tonight, she is boiling with a buzzy anger at me for not playing along in this stupid ass quest.

"I think this one is it," I say pointing to a house with a dim porch light on.

Tanisha had almost walked right past it.

She didn't notice the vases of fake gold roses surrounding the door. They were the opening shot of the documentary.

Even if we didn't watch the movie, if I had to guess where a former rock-star now shut-in black lady lived, this would be it.

In the night, the light purple of the house looks white and dead bushes line the sidewalk.

A waving black gnome with apple cheeks and a chipped hand guards the front door.

One of the windows is yellow with a light still on.

My heart starts hurting again. Like someone pushed a fist into my chest and grabbed hard.

Tanisha looks at the house and for the first time since I've known her, I see her fear. She takes out her phone and starts to scroll, but even I know that she's stalling.

"I'm going to knock," I say.

The only star you can see tonight, shining like its desperate between folds of cloud, is Jupiter. My brother says you know it's a planet and not a star because planets don't try as hard to twinkle.

Maybe tonight Jupiter is a spell because I walk right past Tanisha and even though my heart is a jumpy bird dying all over the place, I step over the spilled water hose and the soft, frayed carpet that says *Welcome* in faded blue, and I rap my bare knuckles on the door.

Once. Twice. Three times.

Nothing.

I'm about to turn back to Tanisha with a *See?*

But then the door opens and it's Betty Davis.

She's dressed like everybody's grandma except she has this dancing fire in her lower lids that bites at everything.

The light hits her hair and forms an orange halo and I don't have words.

She's beautiful and she's older and a little fat. Her hips are snug in her sky-blue velour track suit and she has on a matching robe that hangs on her shoulders like a cape.

She looks like she just stepped out of the ocean.

"What are you staring at girl? Get in."

She turns around and I don't even have time to say anything to Tanisha because Betty Davis has already closed the door after me.

She walks toward her living room.

The lamps are rimmed with something red and heavy. A sleepy white Persian cracks opens its milky eyes and yawns in my direction. Betty's robe billows around her and I follow in its wake.

"Good evening, Ms. Davis," I say, because what else do you say?

"This won't take long," Betty Davis says and sits down, she leans into the plushness of the gold couch and regards me, head to toe.

She doesn't frown or smile, she just sorta lingers, like she's reading me or something.

"No one comes to give," she sighs.

"Maybe I should go get my friend?" I say and wish I had bought her something.

Maybe some real roses.

"That girl will be fine," she says as I sit down on the least flashy piece of furniture in the room, a simple black wooden chair.

"You though, you want answers," she adds.

I wanted the entire world to be outlined like a composition book.

Like how I could make my brother into the person he was before

Iraq.

Or ask why my mom ignores me one day and slaps me the next.

If you saw Betty Davis, guitar between her legs, smile electric, sounding like late night cable sex, you would think, *this is a woman who knows.*

And so I nod and Betty Davis lights a cigarette, blows it out like an old-school diva.

"Well, I aint got shit," she says.

She sits deeper and the couch makes a cough noise, her jeweled hand starts automatically petting the cat on the couch. She pats her thighs with a defiant slap, leans forward a bit and shrugs her shoulders.

This is when I start crying.

I haven't cried in about two years and the sobs scare me.

I reach a corner of my sweater to wipe at my running nose and the snot stretches like a bridge before finally letting my nose go.

I know I'm not going to kill myself tomorrow.

I'm just gonna keep on barely being here.

I'll be the trusty sidekick to the Tanishas of the world.

I'll let my mom hit me until I can leave her house forever.

I'll sneak Darnell's pills back and my brother will keep being the type of screwed up angry who is only nice to me when he's trying to pawn my laptop.

Betty Davis doesn't move an inch, but her eyes become flowers instead of inferno.

I try to calm myself down, breathing deep into the pit of my stomach.

I get up to go, only turn around when I hear Betty Davis stand up. Her bangles jangle. She probably wants to tell me how to unlock the door.

When I'm facing her again, she's so close to me I kinda trip back.

She places her hands on my shoulders like she wants to press me and the words she's about to say into the center of the earth.

I'm close enough to see the thin outline of blue around the brown in her gaze.

Betty Davis' eyes are a planet of churches which pin me to their altar.

"This--is all I've got," she says.

She breathes deep, smiles a bit. And then she's says:

"＿＿＿ ＿＿＿ ＿＿＿ ＿＿＿ ＿＿＿ ＿＿＿ ＿＿＿ ＿＿＿ ."

One day these eight words will swing my legs out of bed when Darnell dies.

A pierced tattoo artist will ink these words on my right forearm when I'm thirty-seven and my mother won't speak to me for three years.

Disgraceful, she'll say.

Betty Davis claps the sides of my shoulders softly and then hands me a CD of her greatest hits from a cardboard box near my feet.

"I don't know what Hue Records thinks I need with 68 CDs of my own damn songs," she says and opens the door for me to leave.

I sneak the CD into my hoody pocket and just like that, I'm outside again in the cold, Tanisha sitting out front.

"She says you can come in now," I say.

Tanisha jumps up like the curb is made of brimstone and runs past.

The door shuts with a soft click.

Minutes later, Tanisha is outside and telling me about how Betty— she's just Betty now—talked about some magical crow and that art is for the brave or something.

We're walking back to the 64 bus stop and I'm a couple of steps ahead of Tanisha.

This time I'm looking at the sky, but there's no Jupiter, just foggy clouds and darkness. In my head, I sing Betty Davis' eight words like a spell and it feels like my feet don't meet the sidewalk.

"You were with Betty longer than me and she didn't tell you anything?" Tanisha asks at my back.

I know this makes Tanisha feel special.

Sacred even.

I turn around to face her.

"No, she barely said a word," I say.

Today I Will Bake a Cake

Layhannara Tep

Today, I did something brave.

After the children left for school and my husband left for his first work interview since we arrived in Beaverton, Oregon, I put on every shirt I owned—three to be exact, one on top of the other. Then I zipped up trousers, because for the first time since we arrived, even I will admit, my sarong was much too thin to withstand the cold weather. Next, I buttoned the wool coat, which according to our sponsor Sue, was a rare find from the church's donation bin. I checked the pockets for any loose change—apparently people do that here—but all I found was a hole in the left pocket and a spare glove in the right.

I fastened a thick cotton hat over my ears, fitted each finger into knitted gloves, and wrapped a scarf around my neck in two loops, the way Sue showed me.

I looked like a swollen noodle, left in the broth a minute too long.

I'd never worn so much clothing in my life.

Before leaving, I counted a few dollars and patted the bills safely in my coat pocket. Then I fished the two most important post-its from my collection in the top dresser drawer. The first was the map Sue drew up for me—directions from the apartment to the grocery store and back. The second spelled out the words 'Betty Crocker.'

Since last Sunday's dinner at Sue's, I couldn't stop thinking about strawberry shortcake.

Soft crumbly bread—the color of lotus petals—and strawberry bits somehow made sweeter by smooth, white cream. Even runny eggs in soy sauce paled in comparison.

And eggs were a delicacy back in Kao-I-Dang refugee camp, where just a month ago, I traded a Thai local a fourth of my weekly rice rations for two precious eggs.

According to Sue, the same eggs that swim in soy sauce are also a base ingredient in cake. Now, when I look at the eggs sitting in the fridge—twelve instead of two—all I can see is the number of cakes they could transform into.

I stared at the grocery list I'd drawn up based on Sue's description—a circle for eggs, a triangle for oil, and a square for the box of cake mix. I crossed off the first two items and knew there was no avoiding a trip to the grocery store.

Before last Sunday's dinner, I didn't even know what cake was.

"We missed y'all at service this morning!" Sue said, as we took our seats around the dining table last Sunday evening.

"The kid…they got homework," my husband pointed to our son and daughter, who looked at him with questioning eyes. In fact, they had spent all morning watching a show called Sesame Street. They repeated the English words that fell from the dolls' gaping mouths, those colorful dolls who never stopped smiling, even when they spoke.

"That's too bad! Pastor John gave a delightful sermon about the last supper."

She nodded toward a painting on the wall, where men the color of Sue were having dinner at a long table. The painting was sandwiched between two wooden crosses, larger versions of the one that dangled from Sue's neck.

"I have a great idea! If the kids ever need any help in school, our youth group has excellent scholars!"

I heard the word 'help' and waved my hand in protest.

"No help."

Sue just smiled and asked us all to join hands while her husband said grace. I looked up while everyone's heads were bowed in prayer, my eyes meeting my daughter's curious gaze from beneath long straight bangs that framed her face like the edge of a cleaver knife. Next to her, my son hung his shaggy head of unbrushed hair, the corner of his lips turned slightly upward, his eyes shut in complete trust.

My husband squeezed my hand, as if asking me to hold my tongue just this once. And maybe he was right. After all, Sue's church sponsored us from Kao-I-Dang to the much safer—albeit much colder—climate of Beaverton, Oregon, where god gave everyone a reason to smile.

He squeezed my hand once more, lest I forget, it was also Sue that came to our rescue last Wednesday.

After dinner, my son and daughter joined Sue's two boys in a game called hide-and-seek, where the "it" person closes their eyes and counts to ten while the others scramble to hide behind the couch, under a table, or in a closet. I would have hidden behind the shower curtains in the bathtub with the lights off— there's no better camouflage than darkness.

I looked over at my husband, whose eyes squinted at the television set as Sue's husband explained what they were watching. Basketball was nothing more than a bunch of grown men running between two sets of nets, trying to throw a ball through the basket. One team wore purple and yellow. The other wore green and white.

If there's anything I hate, it's uniforms. I looked down at my faded blue blouse and tugged at the fabric to remind myself that it's real—the time of all-black clothing was a thing of the past.

While everyone else chatted, I got up and started stacking the plates, until Sue stopped me.

"Please don't, you're our guest! Sit down and enjoy this instead." She handed me a slice of what appeared to be soft pink bread. Strawberry pieces separated each layer and white cream denoted the top layer.

"Thank you."

"You're very welcome." Sue smiled, placing a fork next to my plate.

I scraped off the smallest morsel with the edge of my fork and drew it to just the tip of my tongue. Several bigger bites followed and before I knew it, my entire mouth came to life.

Nothing has tasted this sweet since I last had my mother's taro pudding dessert seven years ago, during what we didn't know would be her last New Year's celebration.

Ma always brought two large pots of taro pudding to temple on New Year's Day—one for the monks and one for anyone lucky enough to get a bowl before the pot ran dry.

That year, just like every year since I was a little girl, I helped Ma prepare the alms bowls for the monks—as she scooped the rice and arranged the vegetables with the runny prahok dip, I ladled taro pudding for each tray.

What got me through the long session of Pali chants was the taro pudding at the other end of the monks' blessings.

Ma only made dessert once a year. Just having one bowl—with warm coconut milk, soft taro chunks, and the tapioca pearl texture— was enough to carry me through the next year.

But on New Year's Day the following year, the Khmer Rouge took over Phnom Penh and 1975 became a year the monks never blessed.

I've always wondered what happened to Ma's two pots of taro pudding dessert that year.

Surely, that morning, Ma must've woken up before the sun rose, as she did every New Year's Day. Boiling taro to its desired softness is a multi-hour process and Ma watched over her pots as she would newborns, one minute, she's fanning the flames to bring the water to a boil, the next she's piling in straw to bring the heat down. When you tend to taro the way Ma did, you draw out the sweetness hiding at its core.

When Ma woke up that morning, she didn't know it would be the first year her dessert would go untouched.

Sue's strawberry flavored bread was not Ma's taro pudding, but it was sweet just the same.

"How?" I asked, when just a few crumbs remained. I pointed to the empty plate in front of me.

"From a box!" Sue laughed and wrote down two words on a yellow post-it.

Bet-ty Croc-ker. She pronounced each syllable slowly so I could write the Khmer pronunciation under it.

She sent me home with a baking sheet pan, a whisk, directions to the grocery store, and instructions on how to use the oven in our new apartment.

On the way out, I clutched the post-its in my left palm. Even if they ended up crumpled, at least I knew they would make it home.

Even with all the clothes on, the cold air slapped my face as soon as I stepped outside.

Sloshy ice fell from the sky and the ground looked like it was covered in coconut shavings.

I felt for my Buddha pendant, where it always rested just beneath my collar bone, underneath all the layers. Along with my wedding band, it was the only thing I carried with me from Cambodia.

Buried at the edge of the garden when our homes were raided, unearthed with each relocation and hidden against the bare skin of my chest, both objects traveled with me from my village, to the labor communes, to the refugee camp, and finally, to Beaverton.

If discovered by the cadres, the ring would have been confiscated—a sister of a classless society had no business holding onto gold.

But the Buddha pendant could have cost me my life—there's no place for Buddha in an equal society.

I rubbed the pendant and whispered a short Pali chant for protection—the same chant I whispered every night on our journey through dark forests, through moist jungle floors, feeling our way to Thailand without a map. I made it then and I will make it now.

The grocery store is only four blocks away.

"You walk straight and take a left at the third block. It should be right next to the McDonald's, remember the golden arches?" Sue used her index fingers to draw two curves in the air.

I'd nodded, even though I only understood a few words. But I'm good with pictures, and so I paid close attention to the map and the symbols she left for me.

"Remember, even if you get lost again, don't be afraid to call. I'll come find you."

But I can't call Sue again. Not after what happened last Wednesday.

I can count the number of times I've cried on one hand, and I'm not proud that last Wednesday was one of them.

What made that day so hard?

It's not like I'm in Cambodia, where just a little over two years ago, a cadre seemed to be breathing down my neck every hour. Work faster. Dig deeper. Plow more. Eat less.

It's not like I'm in Kao-I-Dang, where just a few months ago, a Thai soldier told me I was overstaying my welcome, even as he handed me our food rations.

I'm in Beaverton, Oregon. And all they asked me to do was look for three to four jobs a week and to get the signatures to prove it.

But that Wednesday, after getting shooed away by yet another business owner who couldn't understand what we wanted, I was reminded how some fruit never sweetens. No matter how you till the soil, no matter how many kind words you speak while watering, no matter how many days you wait for the fruit to ripen, some fruit will always come out bitter.

So, for the first time in our lives, my husband and I decided to end the workday before the sun. At 3 P.M., we huddled inside the bus, and I fell asleep against his shoulder. He must've fallen asleep too, because the next moment, we woke up to the bus driver's voice, "End of the line!" And he too, shooed us out.

As we exited, the door closed on my sarong and I had to pull it free before the bus flew past us.

Outside, it was nearly pitch black but for two streetlamps. I looked around and could not recognize the neighborhood. Not one building looked familiar. Not one business. Not even a McDonald's, with the golden arches.

I grasped for my husband in the dark, feeling his shoulder, then the slight bend of his elbow, until I found his hand. I gripped his palm tightly against my own.

"It's okay," he pulled me close with his free arm.

"No, it's not." I shook my head against his shoulder.

"Sure, it's dark. And sure, we don't know where we are. But at least I can take the next step without worrying something's gonna blow up!"

He released my hand and took a few steps forward and a few steps backwards. He did it again and again until I lunged at him, placing both my hands on his shoulders to stop him.

"Don't move!" I shouted. I grabbed both of his hands this time and glared at him in the dark, daring him to let go again.

And then I felt the wetness on my face and thought, *great—now it's raining!*

It wasn't long before I noticed the water was coming from my own eyes.

Realizing his jokes couldn't solve all our problems, my husband leaned in and left slow kisses wherever the tears fell. For a moment, I felt lost in a different way.

It would be nearly an hour before we found a payphone and dialed the number on one of my in-case-of-emergencies post-its.

Even when Sue arrived, the tears did not stop.

She stepped out of her car in a crisp white coat, her hair straight and neat, every strand in place.

"Oh honey." She gave me a hug and patted my head like I was a child.

In her dustless car, I was suddenly aware of the dirt against my sarong and the way the chaotic waves of my hair pointed in all directions. I sat very still. I wanted to leave no traces.

When Sue dropped us off in front of our apartment, she handed me a bible.

"In case you ever get lost again."

So no, I don't think I'll be calling Sue. Even if I can't find my way home.

I followed each step on the post-it and made my way to the grocery store.

I showed the cashier the post-it and she pointed me to aisle five, where I found boxes and boxes of Betty Crocker cake mix.

I brought two to the cashier, ready to splurge. Because even if I only had a few dollars left of our monthly allowance, the sweetness will sustain us.

But when I reached for the dollars in my coat pocket, I realized it was empty.

Of course. There wasn't a hole in just the left pocket. But in the right pocket, where the spare glove had been, was a hidden hole.

Instead of handing the cashier money, I handed her back the two boxes of Betty Crocker cake mix.

She looked at me in confusion until I put down the boxes and pulled out the empty pockets from my coat.

"Tomorrow." I said and turned toward the exit.

"Here, give me those," she said, taking the two boxes, "and take this." She handed me an empty paper bag. "Help me bag groceries and work for tips until you make enough for these two boxes."

I didn't quite understand her, but I took the bag and stood where she pointed at the other end of the cashier station. She placed a glass jar in front of me and said "we bag for tips" to each customer, which prompted them to deposit a few silver and copper coins into the jar in exchange for the filled bags. The customers with the most generous smiles even deposited a folded dollar bill or two.

In two hours, I made enough tips to go home with two boxes of cake mix.

That afternoon, I baked a cake.

Sure, I left it in the oven for a minute too long. And sure, it was a little burnt at the edges. But I covered it in vanilla frosting until it was as white as the ground outside.

No one would know the difference.

My son and daughter walked through the front door just as I finished smoothing over the last layer of frosting.

"Ooo!" My son squealed as he wiggled out of his sneakers and flung his backpack on the floor, practically running toward the kitchen.

"Smells good, Ma." My daughter untied her sneakers before slipping them off and placing them on the shoe rack. Then she picked up her brother's sneakers and lined them neatly alongside her own and hung both their backpacks on the coat rack, before joining us around the cake.

"Can you watch your brother while I run a quick errand?" I reached over to part my daughter's razor-like bangs down the middle, tucking the strands behind her ears to get a good look at her bright eyes. "Your father should be home soon."

My daughter nodded, her eyes fixed on the white frosting.

"Good girl." I said, as I cut three slices of cake and transferred two onto porcelain plates.

I handed each of them a slice before placing the third into a plastic Tupperware container. Then I copied the words 'Betty Crocker' onto a post-it and pressed it against the red lid.

On another post-it, I wrote out the phrase 'No, thank you.' According to Sue, this was the polite way to say no.

I pressed the post-it against the hard black cover of Sue's bible.

Afterwards, I buttoned, fastened, and looped all the layers back on before placing Sue's bible and my perfect slice of cake into a large brown paper bag.

The sun was starting to set, but Sue's house was just a few streets away.

I knocked three times on Sue's front door and placed the paper bag in her outstretched arms.

"Betty Crocker." I said before waving goodbye and making my way back down the familiar road home.

I smiled like the good Christians in Beaverton do.

Last-Last Resignation

Mubanga Kalimamukwento

1st March 2017
Lusaka.

Madam,

Re: Resignation – Prisca Banda

Madam, many months now, you been talking at me, saying, 'Prisca, you need English if you want to be somebody.' You say this last word slow, pounding it into three small pieces that come out with your mouth squeezed like this and your nose pointing up. I take your meaning to be: *If I want to be some-bo-dy, like you, who can make your maid and garden boy scatter to look busy at the sound of your revving Subaru engine, I must add more English to my talking.*

So, with my Christmas bonus last year, I register myself into night school at Lusaka Girls' and start putting somebody-making English into my head.

And thank God, because now I can say my resignation without the trouble of looking in your eyes, which, when they are angry, can chase all the words from my mouth and push them back inside my throat.

This word, *resignation*, I pick it out of Longman Dictionary of Contemporary English in class last week. It mean *'an occasion when you officially announce that you have decided to leave your job,' and 'when someone calmly accepts a situation that cannot be changed, even though it is bad.'*

Last time I am stop this job, it wasn't my own wanting, no. Yourself, you chase me. You call me 'dirty little thief!' of your nice, shining Brazilian wig—the one which you buy on nkongole from Bana Musebo. Even though, when Bana Musebo, she come to pinda you for her monies, I tell her that you fly to Dubai just that morning. In true, you have just run into the pantry, like one of those fat rats which hide behind the sack of mealie meal.

When you finally unlock the door and come out peep-walking, slow-slow, back into the kitchen, with your dress stinking of dry tilapia and your face no more the nice brown of groundnuts but the white of mealie meal, I keep my laugh buried on my inside. I just tell you, 'She's gone, Madam,' and keep on scrubbing the black burnings in a pot at the sink.

You say to me, 'Oh my gosh, Prisca, you're such a lifesaver!'

But one small month afterwards, Madam, you forget all the lifesaving I did by lying on you to Bana Musebo, and dress me in that dirty name: thief.

Thief, it mean to '*steal another person's property.*' Which, if I say the true, I do it sometimes, but only to the cooking oil because my own, it finish too-too fast. Plus, I know if I aks you, you'll just talk me: 'Prisca, you need to manage your salary better!' As if 500 kwacha, it is very big monies which need even to be manage. But your wigs? Never! Me, I like my hair in simple mukule just like this. Yet, even after I explain this, Madam, even after I beat my chest and swear, '*Akalumba fye, Madam, it was not me,*' you still chase me.

'Get out of my yard, you little thief! Don't dare bother me about your salary.' This was you shouting big, squeezing all your face into one tight ball like you ate too much impwa.

Quiet, I pack up my shame and fold it under my arm together with the yellow ShopRite plastic bag where I keep my spare clothes. I carry it out and walk back to Ng'ombe.

Two days go like this, with me having no job. But to tell you the true, it was no different than before, except I spend both of the days at Blessings Maid Centre instead of polishing your floors, and making your daughter Lubuto laugh when ZESCO takes away the electric and she can no more laugh at Disney Junior. I wait there for another Madam to walk in and say, like you, 'You, in the corner. You seem like a hard worker. Come with me!' I wait because I know that I still have enough beans at home to carry my stomach to the month-end. So, the only trouble that worry me then is where I should find the money to give my landlord his rent. But before this problem can press itself into the corner of my eyes and pound my head, my phone ring once.

'Hello, Madam,' I answer.

'Hello, Prisca,' you say, with your voice now butter soft. 'I have no one to take care of Lubuto. Could you please come?'

I know already that you have no one to watch Lubuto because that child takes many days to learn a person's face and longer even, to accept it. I know also that it isn't Lubuto making the butter melt and slide your tongue soft like this. You must have find your wig buried somewhere under the pile of clothes you haven't been able to fit for many months now because your stomach, after Lubuto, it stay swollen like you are too full. This is your *Sorry*.

Lubuto, she is just a baby—only one years, not even big enough for school, and it has only been two days. Too short for her to learn a new maid's face.

'Okay, Madam,' I say, 'I'm come.'

'You're such a darling, Prisca.'

Now, today, you forget the darlingness and put in its place, *pro-stute*. Madam, even for this paper, the word is too ugly. It's still paining me. My chest is still the heavy of cement brick from remembering how you say it so easy. 'I should have known you were just a *pro-stute*, Prisca!'

With your eyes pointing at me straight as if you're talking me something simple like, 'Prisca, bring this to the car, please,' or maybe, 'Check on Lubuto, please, she's crying again.'

The worser thing is, you spit this ugly word in the front of Collins when already, you know, this garden boy has no respect for me. Each time you send me to tell him to water the flower bed, what does he do? He shout, 'Ah, iwe!' even flipping his hand like that, as if I'm his size. 'You're just a kaboyi, like me!' Like his big eyes are blind to see that: 1. I'm a maid who work inside the house and not outside with the dirty, and 2. I am two times his small sixteen-years age.

Worsest, you know me, I pray. You seen me with your own two eyes, wearing my blue-white Dorcus Mother uniform on the Sabbath mornings you bring Lubuto for me to take care of, even though I am off work. How can you now call me a *pro-stute* all because you find that big black pant swinging from the inside hinges of your bedroom door? Big black pant like that, which is not even to my size.

Madam, I beg you, listen me well here, please! That your husband—he was home, yes. For lunch only. I even serve him his favourite: curry chicken with fresh kalembula. I cook it exact the way he want, putting oil at the beginning and again at the end, in between sprinkling crushed chillies and garlic. While he eat, I make myself busy outside, polishing his shoes and reminding Collins to water the roses. Remember you find me on that same verandah? I was putting your husband's shoes to air out the 'five-day stink,' as you say.

Every Friday before this one, you never come home for lunch. Friday is when you get your eyebrows cut into the nice surprise-shape even if it not look like the TV womens. But this Friday, you drive in, rush out of the car and into the house before Collins or me can collect any packages or give you a word. You say, 'I forgot my purse, Prisca—just need to dash in and collect it quick—Lubuto give Mommy a kiss,' fast—fast like that, as if the words are chasing your feet.

Instead of purse, you find your bedroom door open like a mouth—inside it, your husband breathing like a man running, and that black pant stuck in the door like burnt meat between teeth.

It feel like the time start to crawl and then stop sudden when you rush back to slap me. If you are not busy calling me *pro-stute*, I could have tell you that Bana Musebo, she come today. If you are not too busy shouting, 'You little bitch! You bitch! You've been fucking my husband? Shit,' maybe I could have tell you how Bana Musebo, she did not even ask me, 'Is your Madam inside?' She walk into your house, proud on her pointy shoes like this, shaking her buttocks like two ripe mangoes begging to fall from the tree. Like that, she go straight into your bedroom with your husband following behind. Me, I keep myself outside because if I see nothing, I'll have no lies to tell. But even from out there, with the loud of tyres on Independence Avenue, and dogs barking at them through gates, your husband's voice comes running out, shouting, 'Fuck!' for all of Woodlands to hear it.

But, it like, the way your voice climb from alto to soprano quick, scare my own voice. Even when I open my mouth, nothing come out. In my head, I tell you how Bana Musebo, she's tiptoeing out of the kitchen door and through the back gate, holding her sharp shoes in her hands. If you just pause, small-small, between those bad words, I could've maybe point one small finger behind. You could turn your head and see; even the strap of her bra was looking out of her shirt to show you who *pro-stute* is, for true-true.

One last-last thing here, Madam: next Friday, maybe drive home early by small minutes. Twenty minutes, maybe. Enter the house soft. Maybe you catch Bana Musebo before she have a chance to put herself back together. *Coincidence*, say my dictionary: '*A remarkable concurrence of events or circumstances without apparent causal connection.*'

If it don't happen: good! But if it do, allow your tongue to move quick this time, like hot butter in a frying pan. Don't say, 'I need someone to watch Lubuto,' no. Say *Sorry* for true-true, this time.

70

Yours,

Prisca.

The Amaranta Project

Various/Varias

Six selected micro-fictions, in English and in Spanish, in response to Cecilia Vicuña's painting from 1972 "Amaranta." The painting had been "lost and reborn" in 2021 when found.

Awake

Kali Fajardo Anstine

My grandmother once told me I was sleeping my life away. I was soon to be a junior in high school. We stood in her yard about the city's long lined summer sun. I could hear the rattling of my grandmother's antique telephone inside the house. It had a rotary, a dial of numbers. It rang and rang. I once tried unplugging it, but I couldn't find its wall, no end to the cord.

"One day you'll realize how much time you've wasted living in your dreams," she said as we pried yellow dandelions from her square yard on Denver's west side. She was fit for a woman of any age, but especially for a woman in her late seventies. She was spry. Swift. Her pile of dandelions wilted. She had a well-lined face beneath a canvas hat and the skin of her elbows dolloped and grouped as she worked the weeds.

"When you sleep your life away," she continued, pointing at me with her garden gloved pinky, "you miss the world, you go someplace else." She cautiously stood from the earth, slightly bent her back and removed her grass-stained gloves and canvas hat. She kept these things dangling around her, the hat with strings, the gloves tucked into her back pocket.

"Why don't you want to be awake?" She asked.

"What?"

"Awake," she said. "You don't seem to have much interest in this place."

"But I'm awake right now, Grandma." I said, my expression narrowing.

"Hardly," she stated, and turned away from me, heading inside her dusty blue house, the screen door appearing to ripple and bend as she walked behind it.

Despierta

Kali Fajardo Anstine

Traducción de Kianny N. Antigua

Mi abuela una vez me dijo que se me estaba yendo la vida dormida. Pronto estaría en tercero de bachillerato. Nos paramos en su patio junto al largo sol de verano de la ciudad. Podía escuchar el traqueteo del teléfono antiguo de mi abuela que estaba dentro de la casa. Tenía un dial rotativo, un disco de marcar. Sonaba y sonaba. Una vez intenté desenchufarlo, pero no pude encontrar su pared, el cable no tenía fin.

"Un día te darás cuenta de cuánto tiempo has perdido viviendo en tus sueños", dijo mientras arrancábamos dientes de león amarillos en su patio cuadrado, en la parte oeste de Denver. Ella estaba en forma para una mujer de cualquier edad, pero en especial para una mujer de setenta y tantos años. Era vivaz. Veloz. Su montoncito de dientes de león se marchitó. Tenía la cara arrugada debajo de un sombrero de lona y la piel de los codos se le ensanchaba y se le encogía mientras trabajaba en la maleza.

"Cuando duermes toda tu vida", continuó, señalándome con su meñique enguantado, "el mundo se te escapa, vas a otro lugar". Con cautela se levantó del suelo, inclinó ligeramente la espalda y se quitó los guantes manchados de hierba y el sombrero de lona. Mantenía esas cosas colgando a su alrededor, el sombrero con tiritas, los guantes metidos en su bolsillo trasero.

—¿Por qué no quieres estar despierta? —, preguntó.

—¿Qué?

—Despierta—, dijo. —No pareces tener mucho interés en este lugar.

—Pero estoy despierta ahora mismo, abuela—, dije, mi expresión achicándose.

—Difícilmente—, apuntó, y se alejó de mí, dirigiéndose al interior de su polvorienta casa azul, la puerta metálica parecía ondular y doblarse mientras ella caminaba dejándola detrás.

Germinates

Kianny N. Antigua

"The seed has waited"
Cecilia Vicuña

It all started the day the old man invented the tale of the rib; then of biology, of inferiority, of subordination, that of matter itself. Then they confined her, restrained her, sewed her lips together, gouged out her eyes, sat her in a hive of ants, and bathed her in honey. They tied her, oh, they tied her up, with thick ropes and chains and words. They also covered her waist and her sex with iron. They beat her until their own fists began to bleed.

They lit the fires and let the smell of her of burned meat roam the corridors of memory. They cut off her clitoris. They made ablation the norm.

Her head was scraped, they also covered her in black, and sent her for a walk in the desert. They lengthened her neck with copper necklaces and, as a gesture of beauty, mutilated her feet.

All, absolutely all the gods were reconciled to condemn her.

They strangled her.

They killed her over and over again, and over and over again. But the next day, against all expectations and formalities, she grew, her limbs narrowed, her torso expanded, her chest widened, her mouth opened, her tongue saw the light and her voice made itself heard.

She also touched herself, yes, her fingers entered her *geometrized vulva* and she liked herself and she met herself and lived. She then clothed herself with creative blood and resurfaced, with one slash she tore off the strings and after, she germinated.

She germinates.

Germina

"La semilla ha esperado"
Cecilia Vicuña

Todo empezó el día en el que el viejo se inventó el cuento de la costilla; luego el de la biología, de la subordinación, de las limitaciones, el de la materia misma. Entonces la confinaron, la coartaron, le cosieron los labios, le sacaron los ojos, la sentaron en una colmena de hormigas y la bañaron con miel. La ataron, oh, la ataron, con gruesas sogas, cadenas y palabras. Con hierro también cubrieron su cintura y su sexo. La golpearon hasta que sus propios puños empezaron a sangrarles.

Encendieron las hogueras y dejaron que su olor a carne quemada deambulara por los pasillos de la memoria. Le cercenaron el clítoris. De la ablación hicieron la norma.

Le rasparon la cabeza, la cubrieron de negro y la mandaron a echar una caminata por el desierto. Le alargaron el cuello con collares de cobre y, como un gesto de belleza, le mutilaron los pies.

Todos, absolutamente todos los dioses se conciliaron para condenarla.

La estrangularon.

La mataron una y otra y otra vez y otra vez más. Pero al día siguiente, en contra de todas las expectativas y formalidades, ella creció, sus extremidades se estrecharon, su torso se expandió, su pecho se ensanchó, su boca se abrió, su lengua vio la luz y su voz se hizo escuchar.

También se tocó, sí, sus dedos entraron en su *vulva geometrizada* y se gustó y se conoció y se vivió. Entonces se revistió de sangre creadora y resurgió, de un tajó cortó los hilos y luego germinó.

Ella germina.

Answer

Jennifer Croft

The phone was there for rapture; answering it always made her ache. She knew she was supposed to relax like for a car crash, but her hellos were always tense, and whoever was on the other line, and it was usually her father, would always seize upon that tension to espouse his own philosophy, and with each seizure her brain would flash and then get smaller, or less well-connected, maybe that was it, that the more voices you had in your head the worse your head worked, the harder it was to simply be. She was haunted after every conversation by the echoes of people's goals. What she wanted was to go away, maybe to an island, where she could reveal herself to a silent sun and someday, maybe, dance, after drowning out those lifelong rhythms. Letters were better because you read them to yourself. There were even times when she wanted to talk. It was only that the phone was always on the counter, able to spirit her away.

One day she flew to Australia. She understood that there was no such thing as an island. She returned. She felt better in the air, out of reach and already deafened. She learned how to embroider and got a tattoo of a bear eating a dandelion on her shoulder so she'd have something to do in front of the mirror every morning before she went out. Her father got cancer. She moved back home. Afterwards they held a garage sale. She held onto a few of his big button-down shirts. She glared at the phone sometimes, daring it to kidnap her, but now it never rang, and she felt like she was melting, but then she realized she was getting her own rhythms, expansive as the ocean, and she went out onto the balcony and softly serenaded the ferns.

Atender

Jennifer Croft

Traducción de Kianny N. Antigua

El teléfono estaba allí para arrobar; contestarlo siempre dolía. Sabía que se suponía que debía relajarse, como para un choque automovilístico, pero sus saludos siempre salían tensos, y quienquiera que estuviera del otro lado la otra línea, y por lo general era su padre, siempre aprovechaba esa tensión para promover su propia filosofía y, con cada convulsión, su cerebro fulguraba y luego se hacía más pequeño, o menos conectado, tal vez era eso, que cuantas más voces tuvieras en la cabeza, peor trabajaba, era simplemente más difícil ser. Después de cada conversación, quedaba atormentada por los ecos de las metas de las demás personas. Lo que ella quería era irse, tal vez a una isla, donde pudiera revelársele a un sol silencioso y, algún día, tal vez, bailar, después de ahogar esos ritmos de toda la vida. Las cartas eran mejores porque las leías para ti misma. Incluso había momentos en los que quería hablar. Era solo que el teléfono siempre estaba en la meseta, capaz de ahuyentarla.

Un día voló a Australia. Entendió que no existía tal cosa como una isla. Regresó. Se sentía mejor en el aire, fuera de alcance y ya ensordecida. Aprendió a bordar y se tatuó un oso comiendo un diente de león en el hombro para tener algo que hacer frente al espejo todas las mañanas antes de salir. A su padre le dio cáncer. Ella volvió a casa. Posteriormente vendieron sus cosas. Ella se quedó con algunas de sus grandes camisas de vestir. A veces miraba fijamente el teléfono, desafiándolo a que la secuestrara, pero ahora nunca sonaba, y ella sentía que se derretía, pero luego se dio cuenta de que estaba adquiriendo sus propios ritmos, expansivos como el océano, y salió al balcón y les dio una suave serenata a los helechos.

Your Daughter Refashions the Flag into a Crop Top

Rosa Alcalá

The frayed flag of a contested country that barely covered your sex: the thing woven onto you, the thing you had to accept. Yoko Ono put on stage how you knelt and kept quiet, as small, buffoonish men snipped and snipped. You even provided the dull scissors. Vicuña's Amaranta holds a thousand invisible folds of what happened before and after. The original painting and your mother no longer exist, but they've put in a long-distance call to your daughter, who has begun to hear footfalls behind her as she walks around the block. Cecilia once told me she had to choose between poetry and painting, but she no longer believes this and is recovering what was stolen, rejected, lost. You bequeath to your daughter what was left of the flag, and rejecting its unflattering form, she refashions it into a crop top to show off her midriff. She's on the verge of something, that beautiful precipice. On Zoom, her music teacher greets the class cheerily before sharing his screen. But instead of a flute lesson, he mistakenly opens the picture of a woman he keeps on his desktop, undressed. "Awkward!" your daughter writes to her friend in the chat. She tells you she can't remember what she saw, but that doesn't mean he hasn't gotten into her head. "Hombres necios", like bleeding, you are done with them.

Tu hija transforma la bandera en una blusa ombliguera

Rosa Alcalá

Traducción de Kianny N. Antigua

La bandera deshilachada de un país en disputa que apenas cubría tu sexo: lo tejido en ti, lo que tuviste que aceptar. Yoko Ono puso en escena cómo te arrodillaste y te mantuviste callada, mientras hombres pequeños y bufonescos cortaban y cortaban. Incluso proveíste las tijeras desafiladas. La "Amaranta" de Vicuña guarda mil pliegues invisibles de lo que sucedió antes y después. La pintura original y tu madre ya no existen, pero han hecho una llamada de larga distancia a tu hija, que ha comenzado a escuchar pisadas detrás de ella mientras camina por la cuadra. Cecilia una vez me dijo que tuvo que elegir entre la poesía y la pintura, pero que ya no cree en eso y está recuperando lo robado, lo rechazado, lo perdido. Legas a tu hija lo que quedaba de la bandera y, rechazando su forma poco atractiva, ella la convierte en una blusita ombliguera para lucir su vientre. Ella está al borde de algo, ese hermoso precipicio. En Zoom, su profesor de música saluda alegremente a la clase antes de compartir su pantalla. Pero en lugar de una lección de flauta, abre por error la imagen que guarda en su computadora de una mujer, desnuda. "*Awkward!*", tu hija le escribe a su amiga en el chat. Ella te dice que no puede recordar lo que vio, pero que eso no significa que él no se le haya metido en la cabeza. "Hombres necios", como sangrar, ya no aguantas más.

Unfading

Nathalie Handal

Find me in the room midway between life and death, she said. Her hair wrapped in a rope of clouds tied to the sky. Her neck bent by a man's hand, her tongue suspended, one eye hidden, and an old man trying to mine her mind. Men tried to write her for a century, and other eternities. Their head spun in place. **Their rage so loud she stopped hearing it. Telephone wires ran through her body and tugged her in different directions the way exile does.** The way the world falls and the sea begs when love limps. The way numbers climb the wind like death tolls when oppressors are free.

The dead always come alive if they didn't die right. An Andean Condor came and stared. The walls sweating blood. Suddenly they appeared: Sor Juana Inés de la Cruz, Manuelita Sáenz, Juana Azurduy de Padilla, La Pola, Paixáo Pagu, Tania La Guerrillera, las hermanas Mirabal, las Madres de la Plaza de Mayo, las Abuelas de la Plaza de Mayo—speaking the myths, loading their words, and singing songs she **hadn't discovered yet:** *No one will tell you where the water begins in your body nor where the blue gets bluer. It's a question of power. Explore the ruins. Draw the maps of deaths and damages and desires. Dive into her deep. Deep into her erotic. Discover the way back to her dream, your dream, and we will never disappear.* After that, when men tried to strip her clothes off, her sexiness off, her luminance off, she stared at them. An amaranthine stare.

Imborrable

Nathalie Handal

Traducción de Kianny N. Antigua

Encuéntrame en la habitación a medio camino entre la vida y la muerte, dijo. Su pelo envuelto en una cuerda de nubes atadas al cielo. Su cuello doblado por la mano de un hombre, su lengua suspendida, un ojo oculto y un viejo tratando de excavar su mente. Los hombres intentaron escribirla durante un siglo y otras eternidades. La cabeza les dio vueltas. **Su rabia, tan fuerte, que ella dejó de escucharla. Los cables del teléfono recorrieron su cuerpo y la tiraron en diferentes direcciones, como lo hace el exilio.** De la forma en la que el mundo cae y el mar suplica cuando el amor cojea. De la forma en la que los números trepan por el viento, como la cifra de muertes cuando los opresores son libres.

Los muertos siempre cobran vida si no mueren de la forma correcta. Un cóndor andino se acercó y observó. Las paredes sudaban sangre. De repente aparecieron: Sor Juana Inés de la Cruz, Manuelita Sáenz, Juana Azurduy de Padilla, La Pola, Paixão Pagu, Tania la Guerrillera, las hermanas Mirabal, las Madres de la Plaza de Mayo, las Abuelas de la Plaza de Mayo, hablando los mitos, cargando sus palabras y cantando canciones que ella aún **no había descubierto**: *nadie te dirá dónde comienza el agua en tu cuerpo ni dónde el azul se vuelve más azul. Es una cuestión de poder. Explora las ruinas. Dibuja los mapas de muertes, daños y deseos. Sumérgete en su profundidad. Profundo en su erótica. Descubre el camino de regreso a su sueño, a tu sueño, y nunca desapareceremos.* Después de eso, cuando los hombres intentaron quitarle la ropa, su sensualidad, su luminosidad, ella los miró fijamente. Una mirada de amaranto.

Feedback Loop

Nelly Rosario

Maker delivers you in a hermetically sealed, translucent sleeve. In order for you to truly come alive, self-assembly is required. Begin by severing your parts from the packaging (final cut-off from Helping Hand may leave birth wound on left shoulder). For instructions, don't rely on the phone enclosed by Maker. Neither should you attempt to dial the number listed in Manual. (An old man will instruct you to blind your firstborn eye before assembly.) No manual or battery is included save for your own. Disconnect and rewire the phone line. Thread it behind the left breast and through the upper-right chamber of your heart. Breathe. Count. Breathe. Once you feel yourself generating electrical impulses past 100 per minute, direct the gaze of your firstborn eye to the right, diametric to your birth wound at left. At first, you will make out a vision of Self: a tiny, faint, gray figure. Breathe. Count. Breathe. With each impulse, the current your heart siphons from the phone line will render the vision of Self in vibrant color. Your grey tongue will blush, too. When it swells with the metal-sweet taste of saffron, you will know that this vision of Self is real enough to power its own flow. Breathe. Count. Breathe. Self-assembly follows Ohm's Law: Erratic bursts of power will prompt voltage shock in this vision of Self, which will attempt to regulate the current flow by blocking mouth and vagina with hands. Balance the current by aligning your secondborn pair of eyes with the gaze of your firstborn eye, thus rendering a more panoramic vision of Self. The current will flow with regularity between you both. The closer you align your own eyes, the steadier and thicker the current. Breathe. Count. Breathe. Disconnect from the phone line. As the current between you condenses, it will emerge from the vision of Self as a liquid cloth, taking on the color and aroma of amaranth. Using the remnants of the phone line, tether the first of this blood to a loom and swaddle your manufactured body in every thread woven. Breathe. Count. Breathe. As your body is enmeshed in red, watch your vision of Self expand by magnitudes. Align your eyes to her eyes until perspective shifts—you become your own vision of Self. Watch the manufactured body weld to the bloodcloth. From the excess, weave a flag of triumph. You are now Maker.

Círculo de retroalimentación

Nelly Rosario

Traducción de Kianny N. Antigua

Hacedor te entrega en una funda translúcida herméticamente sellada. Para cobrar vida, se requiere auto ensamblaje. Empieza cercenando cada una de tus partes del empaque (el corte final de Mano Amiga podría dejar una herida de nacimiento profunda en el hombro izquierdo). Para obtener instrucciones, no confíes en el teléfono incluido por Hacedor. Tampoco debes intentar, por ningún otro medio, marcar el número de seis dígitos que aparece en Manual. (Un anciano responderá y, con un graznido, te indicará que ciegues el ojo de tu primogénita antes del ensamblado). No debería, de hecho, haber ni manual ni pilas incluidas, salvo las tuyas. Desconecta y vuelve a instalar el cable de la línea telefónica. Enróllala detrás del seno izquierdo y a través de la cavidad superior derecha de tu corazón. Respira. Cuenta. Respira. Una vez que sientas que generas impulsos eléctricos que superen los 100 por minuto, comienza a dirigir la mirada del ojo de tu primogénita hacia la derecha, diametralmente hasta tu herida de nacimiento a la izquierda. Al principio, distinguirás una visión de Ser, que aparece como una figura diminuta, tenue y gris. Respira. Cuenta. Respira. Con cada impulso, la corriente que tu corazón extrae de la línea telefónica hará que la visión de Ser cobre lentamente un color vibrante. Tu lengua gris también comenzará a sonrojarse. Cuando se hinche con el dulce y metálico sabor del azafrán, sabrás que esta visión de Ser es lo suficientemente real como para impulsar su propio flujo. Respira. Cuenta. Respira. El auto ensamblaje sigue la ley de Ohm: las explosiones erráticas de poder causarán inicialmente un choque de voltaje en esta visión de Ser, e intentará regular el flujo de corriente bloqueando la boca y la vagina con las manos. Equilibra la corriente alineando tu segundo par de ojos con la mirada del primero, dando así una visión panorámica de Ser. La corriente fluirá ahora con más regularidad entre ambos. Mientras más alinees tus propios ojos, más estable y espesa será la corriente. Respira. Cuenta. Respira. Desconéctate por completo de la línea telefónica. A medida que la corriente entre ustedes se condense, emergerá de la visión de Ser como una tela líquida, tomando el color y el aroma del amaranto. Usando los restos de la línea telefónica, ata la primera parte de esta sangre a un telar y envuelve tu cuerpo fabricado en cada hilo tejido. Respira. Cuenta. Respira. Mientras tu cuerpo fabricado se enrede en rojo, observa cómo tu visión de Ser se expande en magnitudes. Alinea tus ojos con los de ella hasta que la perspectiva cambie: te conviertas en tu propia visión de Ser, observando cómo el cuerpo fabricado se suelda a la tela de sangre. Del exceso, teje una bandera de triunfo. Ahora eres Hacedora.

Snap This Photo of Two Good Men

Catalina Bartlett

First came the timid knock, followed by their laughter, thin and sugary as capulin jam. I peered through the kitchen doorway, gripping the spatula. Ma was pretending to slap her brother as he scooped her into his arms, twirling Ma until she shrieked, "Stop, 'manito, stop. Por favor."

Tío Domingo looked the same as he did three years ago, except for a blue suit whose pant legs bunched at the ankles and a pair of black patent leather shoes, maybe a toupee. *It's not 1969 anymore*, I wanted to tell him, when everyone in La Puente slicked back their hair and wore thick gold chains, and I did whatever you asked.

They were in the living room, catching up, when Tío said, "JB, you here?"

I pulled back, bringing the spatula to my chest, holding my breath. It was like I'd been holding my breath those three years, ever since I'd scored my first job at that east side convenience store. I was eighteen then and, like my uncle, I wanted women to chase me, wanted to spend money like it was penny candy. Pero, ¿sabes qué? I felt ripped off once I got my first paycheck. Chump change. That's what I got for standing eight hours a day, all that "Yes, sir," and "No, ma'am," and "How can I help you?" When Domingo told me the one-time plan—I would siphon off a little cash each workday, and then on Saturday night, when the money was pouring in, he'd rob the place, doubling our money—I said, "Right on!" without hesitating. We scored once, saw dollar signs, and got our signals crossed the second time. I placed the money in the bag, and he walked out the front door. Just to show off or something, he returned to buy a pack of cigarettes. I'd gotten on the phone a minute before, and soon the sirens were wailing in the background. I rang up the purchase and handed him a pack of Kools. Then he split. The next day, he accused me of calling the cops right before he returned for the smokes. *Vendido*, he told me. I felt a crack in our plans, in us, and I knew it was over. It didn't matter how many times I swore I'd been talking to my bro Teddy, the Viet Nam vet, and not the pigs. Go ahead, I told him. Call him right now if you don't believe me.

"A lo hecho, pecho," my uncle said. That was the first time I'd heard him use that phrase and the last shift the owner told me I'd ever work at the convenience store.

Now Tío was parading around our living room as if I hadn't had to learn to trust in myself and my own dreams all over again. Like buy Ma a house, write songs, play guitar, tour with a band around the Southwest and beyond. Maybe get married and give Ma a grandchild. But Tío still looked good, damnit. Still oozed charm and confidence; still had that swagger. For a nanosecond, I felt an urge to hang out with him again, even though he was dressed like that, and I knew where it would all lead.

Tío strutted into the kitchen. "Well, well, well. ¿Qué onda, Betty Crocker?"

I lifted my free hand, the one without the spatula, in greeting. He moved toward me, but I kept monitoring the egg yolks, watching them harden into yellow Frisbees.

"Johnny-Boy," he said, elongating the "oy" as if it were a shared pet name. "Is that any way to greet your uncle after all this time?"

After the chisme had made the rounds and Tío had split the scene, I'd started over. Took any job I could get, hauling manure, laying sod at the golf course, planting potatoes, until I found my current employer. People had begun to respect me. My hand trembled as I turned up the heat beneath the skillet, praying that the crackle and hiss of frying eggs might mask the sound of his voice, intimate like the guitar in my favorite Roberto Griego song *Un Pobre No Más*. I willed my uncle to leave our casita, even knowing it would hurt Ma to see him go.

My mother appeared in the kitchen doorway. "Hijo," she said, her arms folded.

Domingo held out his arms as if I were his long, lost son. I dug the spatula beneath the eggs and flipped them before reluctantly walking toward him.

"That's right," Domingo said. "That's right."

I almost gut-punched him. But Ma was wearing a hopeful smile, as if this could be some happy-ending story. I stiff-armed Tío Domingo, stuck my hand out like a sword, like Errol Flynn in those old black-and-white movies Ma and I liked to watch. Tío was forced to offer his hand, nothing more. Mine was a firm handshake, the kind I gave my employer. Domingo smirked at me. I nearly choked on the stench of *Terrain*, that shitty-smelling cologne I bought from Woolworth's when I was trying to be like him.

"He's working out at the old Greeves place, Dom. And playing guitar too. Rancheras, my favorites."

"It's no big deal," I said, embarrassed that she was trying to impress him but also itching to grab my guitar and belt out a song.

"He got your musical genius, Connie," Tío said.

"He didn't get it from you," she said.

"I can't carry a tune. But I got other talents, right, JB?" Tío winked at me.

"New ones, I hope," I said.

But Tío had already closed his eyes and was pretending to slow dance with a partner. Was he remembering a lost love in Amarillo or

Denver or Albuquerque? We never knew whether to believe him when he told us where he was going. And we never heard from him until one day out of the blue he showed up on our doorstep.

"Dance with your mother, bro."

He was testing me to see whether I'd become my own man, or if I was somehow still that naïve kid he'd manipulated just because he could. I stood my ground, clutching the spatula, until Ma extended her hand and said, "Juanito." She gave me a familiar look, widened eyes that conveyed a lifetime of waiting on her older brother, even more so now that he deposited wads of cash in her hands during these infrequent visits. There was nothing to do but place the spatula on the stovetop, turn down the heat, and take hold of her. I held Ma as if she were a Saguache cactus, and we moved around the kitchen in a crooked ranchera, Ma singing a made-up Spanish song beneath her breath with words like, No te preocupes, hijo. She spun away from me while I burned inside like a brush fire had swept over me.

My uncle tousled my hair and then yanked it. I swatted his shoulder with the spatula. He grabbed my arm and twisted it. My hand opened, and the spatula flew from it. We all heard the splat of the utensil on the linoleum, and Ma, her back to us, reminded us that we were familia and told us to take care of each other.

"Looks like we're back in business, ese," Tío Domingo said, as burnt-egg odor filled the kitchen. "Just like the old days."

The next morning, we drove west.

"Just to check it out," Tío said about my job. But we both knew better.

We rumbled over the railroad tracks and through the empty streets, turning onto Commerce Boulevard from National Street. The bank towered over us, and the time and weather stats glowed in red on the marquee above the building. We passed Woolworth's, Candelaria Confections, and the Grand Movie Theatre. Soon, my uncle motioned for me to stop at Donut Depot.

Once inside, my mouth watered at the pastries nestled all cozy in the glass case. Tío Domingo had told Ma that he'd stockpiled some money while working. I told him I'd been saving up for a house for Ma, which left no money for luxuries. I bit into a glazed donut. He kept pointing to the donuts, some with sprinkles and others with creamy fillings, and the clerk placed them in a bag.

I elbowed him. "Pay the guy, hombre."

If looks could kill. The flaky donut stuck to the roof of my mouth, and I almost choked on its sweetness. I reminded him about the new house, that every dollar counted. I didn't trust him enough to say I'd saved two grand for a down payment. Domingo glared at me but gave a plastic smile to the clerk who was brushing crumbs from the glass countertop. The doorbell tinkled, and a group of guys herded inside. The clerk gathered their donuts while I chewed on mine, waiting.

He handed the clerk a crisp ten from his billfold, thick with cash. "Next one's on you, kid," he said, elbowing me, as if we were both in on the joke. I doubted he'd ever pay for ten bucks' worth of donuts again. I carried the bag while Tío wiped his hand on his pants. Soon I was steering the pickup down Commerce and cracking open my window. Fresh air filled my lungs, and sugar was rushing through my veins, when Tío said, "You still driving this old jalopy?"

I recognized the movida, payback for putting him on the spot in the donut shop. "You got a problem with that, Domingo?"

"You're bad," he said, holding his hands up. "I don't want any trouble."

"Good answer," I said and gunned the engine.

The pickup zoomed forward. We ate the donuts as the truck engine hummed, and the paper bag crunched each time we pulled a donut from it. We talked about the Denver Broncos and the weather, and then he asked me about the house in the Bow-Wow, a neighborhood named after the wild dogs that once roamed its fields. I told him homes there were being remodeled, Ma had chosen her favorite, and I'd drive him by the house during his visit.

"You're a good son," he said.

"Ma's a good lady."

"That she is, my nephew."

"She doesn't know anything either," I said. "Let's keep it that way."

We passed a mile or two of potato fields before Tío said, "You ever get tired of being a good boy?"

More payback, I guess. Or maybe it was a genuine question. No way of knowing with him. Either way, I gave what I got and said, "Do you ever get tired of being you, Tío?"

"Good one," he said and lit a cigarette, took a couple drags. "You've changed, bro."

"Keep on truckin'," I said, "like the saying goes."

Minutes later, he said, "We did okay, didn't we?"

I thought I heard his voice catch and glanced over at him. "Ya," I said, and I meant it. Sure, there was the rush we'd gotten during the robbery. Afterward, we'd hurriedly split the money while yelling, "Fuck the white honky," and treated ourselves to steak dinners at Sands Restaurant. But the best part? Letting the gringos know in no uncertain terms that we were more than faceless laborers.

The road opened once we passed the A&W Drive-In. I rolled my window down all the way. Nothing cleared the head like the mountain air in the San Felipe Valley. This was the hottest summer I ever remembered, and I'd lived in La Puente my whole life. I always found comfort in the wind, the sway of the Valley's potato and wheat fields, and the mountain ranges that flanked our town on nearly every side.

Tío took another drag and crushed the cigarette butt in the ashtray.

"Just remember, sobrino, you're not the only good guy. Not by a long shot."

I studied him from the corner of my eye. A small paunch rounded out his shirt. His hairpiece was slightly lopsided. None of that mattered when it came to drawing the ladies to him, and I thought for sure we'd be heading to Jake's Billiards or the Blue Bear Pub for that very reason. But the first couple nights, brother and sister had parked themselves on the couch, where they'd spent the evenings smoking and drinking, conjuring the past, and caressing frozen images in framed photographs. One night, after I'd gone to bed, I was roused by Ma's weeping. The two were still sitting on the couch. Domingo was hugging her, and Ma was telling him to save his money. Juanito is doing good, she told him and wiped her eyes with a handkerchief before adding, I'll never forgive his father for making our son become a man too soon. I was glad Ma said what she said, and I guess Tío could act like a good guy when it suited him. Yet I couldn't help but wonder if being good was all there was for me. I left them in a room backlit by black-and-white images of Errol Flynn flashing across the television screen.

"Good to know, Tío. I guess I'll tell Ma you'll be getting a job and sticking around for a while." I pretended to elbow him like I was joking, like when you pretend something isn't serious when it is.

He laughed. "Mira no más. JB, the comedian."

Tío punched me in the arm, I howled in mock pain, and our nervous laughter was swallowed by the wind. The breeze whipped the flame of his lighter, and Domingo cupped his hand around the cigarette. It had felt good to say my piece, like the air had been cleared, and we could drive in relaxed silence.

I turned left onto the road leading to Martinson's farm. Pavement turned to gravel, and a few dogs chased the truck as we bumped along. We were surrounded by mountains. Chamiso, wiry and scrawny, marked the land on either side. We drove by a single-wide trailer whose front lawn was littered with signs that read Coca-Cola or that featured the state flag of Colorado. Soon chamiso gave way to lush fields of wheat. I coaxed the pickup into the u-shaped front driveway, slid the gear into park, and honked twice.

"Let's go," I said and got out of the truck. I angled toward the barn, my footsteps creating a dust storm. Domingo trailed behind me.

Inside the barn, my boss was feeding hay to the horses. Next to him stood Buddy, a large German Shepherd that growled at my uncle.

"I brought a visitor," I said.

Martinson let the hay fall to the ground. I patted Buddy on the back, feeling pride in my employer. He was a fair man who was teaching me to be fair in my dealings with local businesses, whether buying tools at the hardware store or picking up lumber from Gray's.

"Whadda you say, JB?" Martinson pulled off his work gloves and shook my hand. "Looks like you brought reinforcements."

"It's just my uncle," I said, careful not to mention that Domingo had jumped, uninvited, into the cab of my pickup this morning.

The dog stuck close to Martinson and kept emitting a low growl. "Quiet down, Buddy," he said while extending his hand to my uncle. "Theldon Martinson."

Tío told him his name, and they shook hands.

"What brings you to La Puente?"

"My sister phoned and asked me to come." Domingo spread his arms. "Here I am."

"Showing up when called. That's one measure of a man," Martinson said and gestured toward his crops. "JB shows up too, no small thing, especially when it comes to tending to a couple hundred acres of wheat."

I put on my work gloves and lifted bales while Buddy sniffed around me, both of us keeping a wary eye on Domingo. This was only my second summer on the farm, but this was the last job I ever hoped to have.

Martinson called Buddy over to him. "If you got time, Domingo, I'd like to show you around the place."

There's a real gentleman, I thought, someone who could make a body feel at home. I wondered, though, if the old man was being nice for my sake or if he saw something in my uncle that'd escaped me. Maybe Martinson saw some good in a man who never stayed in one place too long, even one drenched in Terrain cologne. I clapped my uncle on the back, and he didn't push my hand away.

As we headed toward the wheat fields, me walking in the middle, a little ahead of them, Martinson started joshing with me. "At the rate you're going, you're gonna own this farm someday."

"I'm gonna be king," I said.

"Whoa," Tío said. "Big talk, young man."

Surprisingly, I didn't hear an ounce of sarcasm in my uncle's voice, and then Martinson said, "Well, now that we're talking." He called Buddy over and said, "Consider yourself promoted, JB. We'll work out the details later."

It came so fast, so unexpectedly, that I could only bumble a thank-you. You earned it, he told me, and I said, "I won't disappoint you."

"We're proud of him," Domingo said.

I couldn't tell if his mouth was curling into that snarl others often mistook for a smile. I wondered whether he could ever be a man like Martinson.

The closer we got to the wheat fields, the more sullen Tio became. Out of nowhere, he asked if I remembered when he'd taught me how to ride a bike. "You weren't more than this high," he said, holding his hand at thigh level. He told Martinson that he, Domingo, had been like a father to me. I clamped my hand over my mouth and pretended to cough, or else I would've burst out laughing. This was a classic Tío move, always having to come out on top, like a shiny penny, Ma once said about him.

But my employer didn't see it that way. Martinson, leaning against a tractor tire, said, "You're lucky. Family is everything, isn't it?"

Tío Domingo agreed with him, and out of respect, I didn't utter a word about Martinson's wife and the rumors of her infidelity. I sauntered over to the tractor whose tires were wider than me and propped myself against one just the other side of Martinson. A bit later, I picked up a stick beneath the tractor and heaved it across the field. "Catch, Buddy." I followed the dog into the wheat fields, leaving those two to fight over me; a cheap thrill, but I wanted to feel it anyway.

By the time I returned, the pair were eyeballing the ground, deep in talk. They greeted me, and we headed back to the barn and then the main house. My uncle surveyed everything—tractors and other farm equipment, a toolbox and assorted tools, animals, acreage—his body heavy with greed, his eyes gulping in all he saw.

"Anyway," Martinson said, once we had reached the driveway, "we could use some help around here if you're looking. It's getting close to harvest time."

"He's already got a job," I blurted. I didn't want Domingo anywhere near the farm, familia or not. I couldn't believe Martinson was that gullible. Maybe that's another reason his wife had left him.

"Thank you for the offer, sir," Domingo said, shooting me a dirty look. "As my nephew said, I'm exploring other prospects. Speaking of which"—and here Domingo inspected his watch—"I'd better get to my next appointment. JB," My uncle looked right at Martinson when he said "JB"—I heard the sarcasm in the slow pronunciation of those two letters—"throw me the keys."

I hadn't bargained on him taking the vehicle. I stood there, rubbing Buddy's head, thinking about how to stall. In the end, I couldn't leave Martinson with a bad impression of my own family. I drew the keys from my pocket and tossed them high and far. "Pick me up at six," I said, as Domingo chased after them.

"Yessir," he said, jogging back, saluting me with his free hand.

Tío Domingo once again shook hands with Martinson. He turned around, keeping his back to the older man as he clapped me on both shoulders. "Keep making our family proud," he said. I was expecting him to press his thumbs into my shoulders, letting up right before I winced, like he usually did. But the hug was genuine, solid. I was not as overwhelmed by the cologne.

He revved the pickup's engine and then rolled out of the driveway. Buddy barked and chased the vehicle to the farm's entrance before trotting back. I looked up in time to see the pickup fishtailing down the gravel road.

I worked harder than usual that day, both to impress Martinson as a newly promoted employee and to shake off the time with Tío. When he was driving away, I was unexpectedly seized by the desire to chase after him and go wherever he was going, like I used to, whatever the outcome. The feeling was fleeting, the size of a kernel of wheat, but I resented that he had this way, just by being himself, of messing with my head, making me want to follow him even when I didn't. I threw myself into cleaning the barn top to bottom and even stayed late to check the center-pivot sprinklers. There was nothing glamorous about farm work, even with the promise of a promotion. By the time I closed the barn door that evening, I'd remembered that Ma deserved a house for all she had done for me, and that I got to keep working at what I wanted most, to be a touring songwriter-guitarist for Los Tigres del Norte or a group like them. These were the rewards of being a good son and staying the course, I guess.

By six o'clock, after Martinson and I surveyed the crops for damage, I was exhausted, and Domingo was nowhere in sight. At seven, Martinson offered to drive me home.

The next day, I learned that Domingo had spent the entire time at Jake's Billiards. There would be no job offer. This knowledge left a taste in my mouth as sour and stale as the alcohol and cigarette smells that clung to our walls. I forced myself to vamoose by six every morning to avoid seeing him. All week, I shut myself in the bedroom and practiced guitar, imitating the plaintiveness of Roberto Griego's ballads, writing my own lyrics in a spiral notebook, imagining myself performing my songs and wailing on guitar on stage. Eventually, the clang of pots and pans would invade my music-making. I'd place the guitar in its case, go stand next to Ma who was all alone and hunched over the sink, and afterward, set my alarm for work the next day.

A week or so after Tío Domingo's arrival, I slipped into the cool air at the usual time. The sky was dark. Domingo and Ma were asleep. I opened the truck door.

"Boo," Tío said.

I jumped back, nearly falling over.

"Pendejo," Domingo said. "Pay attention."

"You scared the hell out of me." I straightened my chaqueta. "You can't go with me."

"Martinson invited me."

Domingo, like the rest of us, had what was called selective memory, something I read about in the psychology magazines delivered each month after Ma had won some contest. You remember the shit that makes you look good and conveniently forget the shit that makes you look like a jerk. Maybe that's why Domingo spent so much time at Jake's—its dark interior washed away the bad, making him a winner all the way around. For him, each moment could be fresh, as if the past had never happened the way it did.

I turned the key in the ignition, "You left me hanging the first night. Do you think Martinson would forget that?"

Domingo shrugged. "That ain't nothing I can't fix"—and he snapped his fingers—"like that."

"It's manual labor, Domingo. Surely someone like you has better ways to earn money."

"For once, you're right, kid." He lowered his voice. "I got this idea. We can make big money and leave this hellhole."

"What in the hell are you talking about? Ma would never leave the Valley, and I'll never leave Ma. You know that."

"We'll bring her, too. She'll get over it. You want more money, don't you?"

"Everyone wants more money," I said, which Tío took as permission to tell me the whole plan. Afterward, I said, "I'm not screwing over Martinson."

"He's part of the system, kid. You'll strike a blow for gente all over the world."

Yes, I'll do it, I wanted to say, for people like me who wanted something that purposely had been put beyond their reach. Listening to him, I couldn't help but feel that old tug again, that desire to hit the gringos in the wallet where it would hurt them the most.

I pumped my fist in the air. "¡Viva la raza!"

"That's it, kid. You've got it."

"I'm practicing."

"For what?"

I looked over at my uncle and said, "My speech to the pigs when they throw my ass in jail for your pendejadas."

Domingo whistled. "You almost had me, kid," he said as he shook his finger at me. "But like I said, just leave the barn door open one night, and I'll do the rest. Your skinny ass won't even be involved."

I drummed my fingers on the steering wheel. Back then Tío had said that white people had screwed us out of our land, our history, our memories. *They owe us.* I'd said. *Fuck them.* He'd said, *Simón, ese.* I still meant it. That's what it meant to me to "screw the system," as my uncle put it. I told myself I was just going about it a different way now.

I changed the subject. "Let's go see the house, Tío."

"It's your deal, bro. I'm just along for the ride."

"I promised you anyways." Maybe seeing my future, and his sister's, would change his outlook on this bizarre scheme.

I turned off Commerce, and the truck dipped down a hill and bumped over the railroad tracks. We were in the Bow-Wow, but Tío Domingo seemed lost in thought. I parked across the street from the house. "This is it."

He looked at the house, and I tried to see it as he would. Beige stucco shaped like a square, blue trim, a fence of concrete blocks around the front yard, patches of dried grass for lawn, some rusted car parts, a couple cottonwoods.

Domingo sat there for a long time without speaking. I told him we were almost ready to make the move.

"It's nice. A real home. Connie made a good choice."

I thought I heard something new in his tone. My uncle had never said a word after my dad left. I had no proof, but I always believed he'd never forgiven my father for breaking his sister's heart and making her own living conditions worse, and mostly, for forcing him, someone who could not settle down, to be the only reliable man in her life.

I put the truck in gear and drove back the way we came, veering left onto the main drag on the way to Martinson's.

Not two minutes later, my uncle picked up where he'd left off. "He won't even know the toolbox is missing. Just do what I said, and you'll be out of it after that."

The toolbox was bright red and made of steel, the size of a large chest of drawers. Its ten compartments were filled with expensive tools. All of it was worth my savings and a couple of Ma's paychecks combined.

"I suppose Martinson won't hear you haul it away in the middle of the night either."

"He won't be there."

"He lives there, wise guy. It's his farm."

"One of the guys at Jake's overheard Martinson say he was leaving town for a few days."

"I haven't heard about it."

"You're a hired hand, bro. Don't ever think you'll ever be more than that."

Damn. I wished Tío could see that I was worthy of respect. *Who cares what people think, hijo?* Ma always said. *I don't,* I always told her. But Tío Domingo needed to remember that I worked for one of the most admired men in the Valley, that I had just been promoted, that my word was as good as the old man's. All this made me someone who was admired too, and that was a righteous feeling, better than any two-bit con job.

I parked in front of the donut shop. This time I offered to pay, but he held up his hand, and soon I was watching him through the storefront window. The guy had been replaced by a cute girl. My uncle was all más suave, putting on a display just to make a point. But I had other things on my mind. What if I was playing into this white man's hands? What if I'd settled for a low-level job with only a promise of a future, no matter what the old man said? What if I was being screwed over by the white man, and I didn't know it?

Domingo returned with coffee and a baker's dozen. "Fringe benefits," he said and winked.

"This is the last time, bro, I swear," Domingo said after licking icing from his fingers. "I just need to straighten a few things out, and I'll be out of this business forever."

I watched the sun rise while munching on a glazed donut. "Martinson knows everything that goes on. You think he's an idiot?"

"He's no idiot. But he's not as great as you make him out to be either." Domingo stressed how much money the toolbox and the tools were worth. "This chance won't come again."

"Okay, okay, Tío. I get it." Any fool could see it made no sense to blow up my life again, but Tio was wearing me down. I honestly was afraid I'd say yes just to shut him up, if nothing else, and then Ma and I really would be screwed. I slammed on the brakes in the middle of Commerce, across from the A&W Drive-In.

Coffee spilled onto Domingo's lap. "What the hell!"

"Get out of my pickup. Now."

"Cálmate, kid."

I leaned over and pushed him toward the door. "You heard me. Get out."

"Don't touch me, motherfucker." Domingo got out and slammed the door. "Just another coconut. That's you, white boy."

I screeched down the highway. Glancing in the rearview, I saw him cruising toward the restaurant, as if it were an ordinary day. The steering wheel was shaking, and I forced my hands to stop. By the time I turned onto the gravel road, I'd cooled down. Martinson was out on the tractor, so I tended to the horses. Maybe the promotion was on his mind because Martinson called me over and explained that the wheat crop had dried to a reddish-gold and was nearly ready for harvest. He broke off a seed-head and rubbed it between his hands to release the seeds, a few of which he dropped into my palm. We each bit into one and they were crunchy, indicating a ready crop. Martinson said he would reveal the next steps in due time. That afternoon, surveying fields of near perfect wheat stalks, I felt something inside me become firm.

Martinson turned to me and said he had some business to take care of in Denver.

My stomach tightened, recalling what my uncle had told me. When Martinson asked me to watch the place in his absence, saying he'd pay double, I almost puked on the wheat. "You can bunk in the spare room," he said, pointing toward the house. He added that Troy, a farmhand from Albuquerque he'd hired a couple seasons back, would stop by every day to help. I didn't know who this Troy guy was, but I almost hugged my boss in the middle of the wheatfield. *Take that, asshole*, I said silently to Tío Domingo as I shook Martinson's hand.

The room was spare but clean, like the rest of the house. There was a twin bed, with a white bedspread and a single pillow. Ma had pressed some extra shirts, which I hung in the closet. Jeans, boxers, and t-shirts fit in the drawer of a small wooden dresser. Martinson had said, "Make yourself at home, JB." But I felt awkward filling the refrigerator with the food Ma had packed: bear claws, bologna, a gallon of milk, cokes. My bag of potato chips, loaf of Wonder bread, and Cap'n Crunch cereal box looked out of place on the counter.

The other rooms were tidy like mine, though the door of the master bedroom was locked. Maybe it was filled with his wife's belongings because the rest of the house was forest quiet and empty. There were no photographs, no sign that anyone lived there. I prided myself on staying out of my employer's personal matters, so I shut the front door and headed to the barn. I also hadn't mentioned anything about this gig to Domingo, and I'd even sworn Ma to secrecy.

Opening the barn door, I half expected to see my uncle, and was relieved to find horses staring at me with their mournful eyes. I slipped the feed bags over the horses' snouts and went about the daily chores. I was checking the fruit trees when a pickup chugged into the driveway. Out jumped this stranger.

"How goes it?" he said.

I stood up, wiping my hands on my jeans. This had to be the worker that Martinson had hired a while back. *Who is he?* I'd asked that afternoon. But Martinson was charging into the fields, complaining about the irrigation system for the wheat, and the question was left hanging in the air.

I introduced myself and told Troy that I'd show him around. Walking ahead of him, this younger-looking version of my employer, I asked him how he knew Martinson. Me and a friend worked here a while back, he told me, and figuring I'd never get more than that, I rushed ahead and arrived first to the barn. I turned to make sure Troy was still with me. If anything, he'd slowed down to a stroll, as if he was on vacation in the tropics or some other place I'd never been. I stifled my envidia as I watched his easy gait and his unruffled confidence, as if he'd been born with it.

We went inside where Troy proceeded to check out all the equipment, the livestock, everything. A vague feeling of déjà vu tugged at me, but I brushed it away. I was paranoid about my uncle and reminded myself that not everyone was like Domingo. It was my second day on my own here, and already I'd grown weary of jumping at every creak and groan that the wind made happen.

By the end of the afternoon, we'd strung a barbed wire fence around the field to mark the land's boundaries. Martinson had received reports of the neighbor's errant cows crossing onto his land, and both owners had chipped in for materials. I was glad for the help and the company, and I said as much to Troy.

"Just doing my duty," he said, climbing into the cab of his pickup. I returned to the task of figuring out how to prevent mice and rabbits from chewing the bark off the few apple trees in the small orchard behind the main house.

I bunked in the barn the first couple nights, just to keep a closer eye on things. But I slept poorly, and my work suffered the next day, so I took up residence in the guest room that Martinson had prepared for me. Troy came by every day, and together we lined the gravel driveway with rock, shoed one of the horses, and planted marigolds and bacopa to discourage ravenous deer.

Ma called during that time. No word from Domingo. I was sure my uncle hadn't forgotten, but maybe too many late nights at Jake's made it impossible for him to face the long, hot days. Maybe he'd gotten the message that I'd either banish him or hand him a shovel. I played my guitar, chuckling at the thought of Tío Domingo digging holes for fence posts. Relaxed, I fell asleep fully clothed on the twin bed, the guitar resting on my chest and Buddy running around outside.

If it hadn't been for my guitar, I would have slept through that night. I must've rolled over, which sent the instrument thudding to the ground, sounding its discordant twang. I leapt out of bed and nearly stepped on it.

"Buddy," I called, but the dog didn't come.

I grabbed a glass of water and looked out the kitchen window. A light was burning in the barn. "Damn it," I said, and threw on some clothes, then ran toward it. I pulled open the door. Troy's pickup was backed into the building, and he was standing in the truck's bed. At first, I was relieved. The guy must have left something or had come back to finish a job. But then I saw the head of black, shiny hair near the back of the pickup and Buddy muzzled with duct tape.

"Cabrones," I yelled.

Troy jumped down. "We're loaded," he said and gave the truck a double slap.

I shut the barn door to prevent him from leaving and ripped the duct tape from Buddy's muzzle. The dog leapt for Troy, barking and trying to tear at him. I grabbed the nearest thing to me, a rake, and went for Troy who by then had kicked the dog and jumped into the driver's seat. I lunged for him, aiming to gouge him with the rake's tines. But he shoved me back and took off in the pickup, the red toolbox and tools tied down in the back.

I had barely gotten up when Domingo came toward me, looking stoned out of his mind, his hair flapping back and forth across his head. When he was close enough, I swung as hard as I could. The punch landed in his gut, where I'd wanted to place it on that first day at the house. He staggered, and I reached for the rake, which had fallen a few feet from us. Domingo had the same idea, but I knocked him out of the way and got there first. Holding it in front of me, I said, "Go ahead, you pinche coward."

Something inside him blew up, and he threw himself at me. I stepped back, tripping over a flashlight or something. Down went Domingo and then me. I couldn't get up fast enough, and Domingo was on top of me. I pushed him off me using the strength that working on the farm had helped me build. I managed to push him down and jump on top of him. I let loose, punching and screaming, even scratching. He tried to gain the advantage, but I was a wild man, unrecognizable even to myself. "Holy shit," Tío Domingo said when he couldn't recover his stance. His breath smelled of beer and pot. I gut punched him again, putting all the anger I'd been holding since my father had left and my uncle had unceremoniously waltzed back into our lives. We wrestled, spit spraying, arms flailing, legs pushing, grunting and groaning. I managed to pin him down until I felt his body go slack, and I knew I'd won. Then I walloped him once more for old time's sake. We lay on the barn floor, our chests rising and falling. He was too sore, too tired to move, but I felt like going another three rounds.

I pulled myself to a sitting position and saw Domingo patting his head. I thought he had cracked his skull or something. But then he fell to his knees, and I realized he was searching frantically for the hairpiece, that sad-ass pelt.

"Hey, pelón," I said.

I laughed until tears rolled down my cheeks, bits of hay flying from my mouth like tiny streamers. Domingo started laughing too. I left him there and headed to the house. When I looked back, he was still crawling through the hay. Let him follow me for a change. I found Buddy, went back to the house, and sat in Martinson's chair on the porch. Domingo made his way over, holding the toupee, and I didn't help him. He lowered himself onto a nearby stool. I went to the kitchen and grabbed a couple glasses of water plus a bottle of aspirin. After swallowing the aspirin, he placed the fur rug on his leg and pulled a joint from his pocket. He lit the joint and inhaled. I nodded, and he passed it to me. We went back and forth until the joint became a roach.

"Last toke," Domingo said and handed me the butt. "You're never too good for la marijuana, bro."

Afterward, I staggered into the house, and Domingo followed me. We gobbled two bowls each of Cap'n Crunch cereal. I filled two more and placed one in front of him.

"You won't rat me out, will you?" Domingo said, spooning cereal into his mouth.

That question had glowed beneath every utterance, every laugh, each time my fist connected with Domingo's body. I'd been mulling the answer since I'd opened the barn door, while we smoked grass, now that we had the munchies. I'd even dredged up a rare memory of my father, his sadness when I preferred to sit and sing songs instead of joining him and Ma in the potato fields. I couldn't admit to myself, much less to Domingo, how much it had meant to me to go out on jobs with him as an equal partner, not a kid, how much I still longed for that.

"I'll be talking to Martinson tonight."

Domingo slapped me on the back. "What would your mom think about that?"

"You made the same promise, Domingo, that we would take care of each other, which includes her."

"Blood is thicker than water, bro. Always."

"You're not free and clear. Like I said, Martinson will be back tonight."

Domingo snorted. "You'd choose a gringo over your own uncle?"

"Don't put this on me. Come clean, and we'll work it out. Troy too."

"Don't worry about Troy." Domingo flicked the cigarette butt into the dirt. "Loan me the pickup and we'll come for you tomorrow."

"You're on your own. And so is Troy if that's even his real name."

"I'll see you around, bro." He stood and pointed to his head. "Don't tell anyone about the piece."

"Ya, sure," I said.

"Nephew," Domingo said.

I looked up.

Domingo stood at attention, his fist raised. "¡Viva la raza!"

The black patent leather shoes bobbed up and down as he meandered down the dirt road. I returned to the barn and plopped onto a bale, nuzzling Buddy and trying to figure out how to explain the missing toolbox to Martinson. I'd made no promises to my uncle, told him I'd snitch. But if I told Martinson the truth, would the old man believe me? Would I still get that promotion once he saw the space where the toolbox had been?

I glimpsed a bright light outside and thought Domingo had had a change of heart. Relieved, I petted Buddy. "Let's see who's there," I said and opened the barn door.

The wheatfields illuminated the sky like a fireworks display gone haywire. I lurched toward the fire. The flames singed the hairs on my arms and head. I hauled myself back to the house, coughing and spitting up, and dialed the firehouse. There was a sprinkler system, I remembered finally, and my hope of saving those golden fields was revived. Later, piecing together the night's events, I would come to understand that Troy hadn't been watering the wheat enough each day, and the sun had dried the earth irredeemably. I would figure out that my uncle had flicked a couple lit cigarettes into the wheatfields, that he and Troy likely had doused the fields with gasoline beforehand. The suspicion of arson to collect the insurance money would cling to Martinson like wet, burnt wheat stems, and I didn't know then that this same suspicion would cling to me. At the time, and forevermore, I pictured Tío Domingo and Troy heading north in the truck, passing a joint between them and laughing their asses off, caring only about themselves, about getting back at me, not giving the slightest thought to Ma and what she had lost.

In that moment, I felt only terror, followed by a nauseating pity for me and Ma, doomed to live forever in our sad, cramped rental on the southside. Everything—the house in the Bow-Wow, this and possibly any job, the income, our savings, those years of clawing my way back to respectability, and most of all, the respeto itself, all of it gone. I dropped the phone, ran outside, and turned on the spigot. Water flushed from the hose. I dragged it toward the wheatfields, as fire engines screamed down the dirt road.

Quimbamba

Yolanda Arroyo Pizarro

Translated by Lawrence Schimel

I.

The plain truth is that was the bitch's name: Quimbamba. My brother showed up at the house one afternoon explaining that his ex-girlfriend had given her to him as a pet. We looked at him unbelieving, but in silence. We've mistrusted my brother's stories for a long time now, since they seemed invented to us, especially those that included imaginary girlfriends. For various reasons that aren't worth getting into right now, we didn't say anything nor contradict him. We reacted with fake astonishment, something that didn't make him feel any shame or embarrassment. We pitied him so we let him get away with it, especially after the beating he got at school.

However, I knew the indisputable truth that my parents were unaware of. The dog was a stray, abandoned, a runt. My old group of friends and I had burned its tail not once but twice. And although that had happened a long time ago, if you looked carefully, you can still see the tip of its tail was still charred, the poor thing. My twin—so different from me in his weakness and his sensibility, he so loved poetry that they called him *palesiana*, and was such a fan of *culpiandeo* and the graceful undulations of Jennifer López's hips (when my parents weren't looking, he'd imitate her)–announced triumphantly that the dog's name was Quimbamba. I almost snorted the soda I was drinking out through my nose, but in the face of this, his new invention, I didn't say a word.

Papá and Mamá, who already planned the *mudanza criolla creativa*, opposed his having a pet on principle. And I say that about the move like someone deciding to baptize a process as unorthodox as that one was. Moving from the Island should be an easy thing in itself, but moving in the way so many boricuas did it, that was something else entirely. Some called it the *proyectazo*, the grand project. The procedure had to go like this: first, pack the minimum of clothes, shoes and things, as if we were going to return to the island from a long holiday; two, stop making the mortgage payments (the more months, the better); three, stop making payments on the only car we had left after the sudden sale of Mamá's (and again, the more months unpaid, the better); four, in the end, let them cut off the cable TV, the electricity, the water supply, and any other monthly service. Having bad credit is the least of it, I heard them say a few months ago to an aunt who'd already gone. They claim that in the United State they'll give you a house, a car, and utilities even if your credit rating is so low it's underground. Finally, use the little money that came in to buy the necessities, get the airline tickets, and save for our new life. Although my parents had been laid off due to the financial crisis, their unemployment checks, the food coupons, and the jobs Papá and Mamá did under the table kept bringing in some cash.

We were to go live at first in the house of that cabrón, uncle Félix, and then, when we began to have the small fortune that Papá would manage to amass, we'd buy our own house with an American pool and a few cars. Because in *Niuyor* everything is better, and Orlando is, without a doubt, the best part of *Niuyor*. When I say that uncle Félix is a cabrón, that falls short as a description, because a few years ago my twin already accused him of touching him in places he shouldn't. So the fact that we need to go live in the lion's fucking cave is just surreal. But that's what familia is for, Papá always says, to help us in our worst moments. After which, we all bite our tongues and keep quiet. All of us except for Quimbamba, who decides to unexpectedly bark her head off, as if my twin had told her everything and she'd understood, and this were part of her protest.

My twin took care of Quimbamba all day, somewhere that wasn't our house. When he returned in the afternoon or evening, he came back with her having already eaten, drunk, and taken care of her business. Both of them slept together on the same mattress. The dog had a collar that my brother claimed another ex-girlfriend had given her. It had the colors of the rainbow and said in big letters QUIMBAMBA. That damned bitch hadn't forgotten me. She hates me. She barks at me every now and then, growls at me, bares her teeth at me whenever nobody is watching and I suddenly stretch my leg and give her a kick, which she responds to by howling and running away.

Part of the procedures of the *mudanza criolla creativa* (regulations already perfected earlier by other neighbors and which we follow because that's what one does) entailed selling off the belongings and furniture of the house little by little, even if those were still being paid off to the furniture store or the loan house. What was most important, I heard Mamá say, is that the last thing to be sold should be the fridge and the washing machine, for obvious reasons. And I say the last as someone who's spent entire weeks now sitting on the floor in a living room without a sofa, without chairs, without stools or pictures on the walls, without vases or coffee tables or a television. The oven, the microwave, the dryer, and the beds were all gone. We slept on a mattress on the floor which left our backs aching and we heated canned spaghetti on the little gas cooker that we used during blackouts, whether from a hurricane or not. And although our parents begged us to keep going to school so as not to raise suspicions, the truth is that my twin and I go if we feel like it and otherwise don't. Almost always, he goes off to the house of his friend and I spend it sitting in a corner of the mall without bothering anyone, watching *Kill Bill* or *Django* on my phone. I love those films. Besides, it was almost summer so going to class didn't matter, so I sometimes observed the girls who passed before me. I fantasized about them, as if I knew them or held their hand... possible imaginary girlfriends, perhaps.

II.

The day we were finally going to move, we set the alarm so it would wake us really early, that way we'd leave for the airport with plenty of time and follow the instructions of the *mudanza criolla creativa*. The sun was barely showing its orange and pink tones when we notified the security guard of our urbanización that we wouldn't be returning. He phoned some cousins with a pick up truck and they'd take care of removing whatever remained inside the house and the garage, to resell it. Depending on how much money they managed to make off that sale, they'd send us a commission to our new address, that way we all helped one another. When the people from the bank, the loan house, or the furniture store came to try and repossess the properties or goods, they'd find themselves with the surprise that little or almost nothing remained, barely the structure itself. Although not even that would be a surprise, I guess. We just joined a mechanism that had been happening the same way for years already.

In the car, my twin and I travelled in the back seat in silence, as if we were upset. The dog was at his side, stuck in a special suitcase-bag that another girlfriend had given him. He opens his mouth and whispers so only I can hear him: *the first time that cabrón tries something, I'll cut his throat.* He says it and lowers his face. I can almost see the tear that doesn't fall from his right eye. I hold his hand and answer: *And I'll cut him to bits if he dares touch us again.*

The car is left in the airport parking lot with a purple piece of paper that Papá places on the front windshield. That lets the employees who are "involved" know that the car will remain there without an owner. Anyone could use it without giving it back to the bank, those bourgeois pigs have enough money already. Some hired hoodlum would come collect it, finding the keys hidden in one of the tires. It would be sold in pieces or the plates changed to be used in some heist.

III.

I don't manage to make friends in this little neighborhood where everyone speaks boricua. I feel very alone. I'm an odd girl, introverted, who amused herself burning the tails of vagrant dogs and who soon discovers that in this state of the great American nation there aren't any. Neither dogs, nor friends, nor vagrants. The streets are clean of trash and people. The cars are not left parked in front of the houses, but inside the garages. The yards have their lawns neatly cut and manicured. Although it's June, I've started to attend a new upper school to take English lessons. My twin, unlike me, has already made great friends who seem to understand him and accept him without a girlfriend. No beatings can be spotted in his near future. In secret from Papá and Mamá, he starts going with his friends to parties with colored wigs in disco clubs. That's why the news catches us by surprise. That's why we feel such desolation and confusion at what happened.

No one prepares us for it.

IV.

It is the celebration of the Noche Latina. They explain to Papá and Mamá that some nighttime joint gets chosen, sometimes an open-air bar, and some bands or DJs enliven the whole night long with music by Marc Anthony, Celia Cruz, Gloria Estefan, or Shakira. And even by Ricky Martin. That night, the party is at a club called Pulse.

Then the bullets. Then the running, running. The shouts. The friends who try to save one another. The mothers who serve as a human shield so the shots don't reach their children. The fathers who leave behind so many orphaned boys and girls. The sound of the machine gun and the police, the FBI, the helicopters. The TV and radio station transmitting everything live. Some already talk of massacre, of dozens and dozens of dead and wounded. They narrate the exploits of some trying to escape; the wails, the prayers, the insults of others. The body count: twenty five, thirty two, forty nine... I am not there. I find out about everything from a live broadcast on my phone. Gripped, speechless, frozen in place staring at the screen.

Later I'm witness to the phone call to our home by the hospital staff. Later, I see my parents answering the calls that follow from the morgue.

In our house, even that cabrón uncle Félix is wailing.

I look at Quimbamba and her collar with the colors of the rainbow.

That damned dog still hasn't forgotten about me. She hates me. She barks at me, growls at me, bares her teeth as if asking after my brother. What can you do if the being who you came into the world with is no longer there now? What can one do with this abyss that turns distance into eternity? How can one console oneself knowing that the heart that beat alongside your own inside the womb no longer exists?

Quimbamba barks. She growls. She bites me and blood wells. Then I reach out a hand and grab her. I embrace her too tightly. I almost smother her. I squeeze so tight she howls and it's only then that I realize that it's both of us who are howling.

The Wall

Sabahattin Ali

Translated by Aysel K. Basci

For a long time, I stayed in a prison by the sea surrounded by ramparts. The noise of the waters striking those thick walls echoed through our cells, which were made of stone, and invited us to take a long journey. The seabirds hovering above the ramparts with their wet wings looked at the iron fences with eyes blinking in amazement, then immediately flew away.

Shutting a prisoner in a place with no connection to the outside world is doing him the greatest of favors. In fact, there is nothing more devastating for a prisoner than to know he is so close to freedom, he could touch it with his hands, and yet he is so far away from it. What a torment it is to listen to the sea, only ten feet away, knowing it's a door to freedom. But instead of being free, you cast your eyes endlessly at the thick ramparts separating you from freedom and see the sea only in your imagination. Isn't it better to be locked up in a place where the only thing that reminds you of freedom is your breath? That's better than watching a bird in a prison garden eating breadcrumbs at your feet, walking around left and right on the same soil without liberty, and then, with a flap of its wings, it soars beyond the walls and embraces freedom?

Ironically, at the prison in which I was incarcerated everything, even the noises, were designed to bring freedom right in front of our eyes. Then we would watch it abruptly evaporate. Because I was a prisoner, whenever spring was in the air, the small trees growing on top of the ramparts and the yellow flowers drooping from the mossy stones covering those walls filled me with grief. The small white clouds gliding like swans across the endless sky took away the only consolation I had: forgetting. And yet here, everything the prisoners talked about was related to the past and the outside.

It was as if nobody lived after arriving here, or their memories were no longer retained. When it was necessary to talk about life inside, it was described with such reluctance that the listener was tempted to stop the conversation to end the suffering of the one talking.

An exception to this involved a grey-haired prisoner, who told me about an incident that had happened to him when he first arrived here. Perhaps the reason he was able to describe the incident without hesitation was because it was related more to the outside than inside. This was the story of a failed escape attempt.

But let's first talk about the walls of this prison:

The courtyard was surrounded by ramparts on all four sides, but on the only side connected to the land, there were multiple consecutive walls, and they were much thicker than the rest. Centuries ago, this place was the city's interior palace. In those days, young odalisques (female slaves) in the garden probably listened to the sounds of the waters and looked at the sky hopelessly with the same longing for freedom as they too wandered around. These thick walls were constructed to hide them from strangers' eyes and to protect them from enemies. Today these slaves have been replaced by bearded, pale-faced, miserable men, totally disconnected from the rest of the world.

Now, the western corner of those walls, partly collapsing and fully covered with weeds, was being demolished. There were rumors that new, single-occupancy prison cells would be constructed there.

One day, I was watching the demolition together with that gray-haired prisoner I mentioned earlier. We were looking at many pieces of mortar falling as workers hammered the wall with their pickaxes. It was taking a long time to demolish the wall, which was eight meters wide, and those prisoners who were allowed into this part of the outer garden—those considered trustworthy from a security standpoint or who had been there for many years—were watching the activities from morning to evening with great interest as this was very rare "entertainment." The wall was half demolished when the grey-haired prisoner, who until then had been standing quietly next to me, bent down and whispered in my ear:

"Once I was going to escape from this wall."

I looked at his face curiously. He walked toward a dried quince tree at one edge of the garden. We crouched down next to one another and he started to explain, without moving his eyes away from the pieces of falling mortar:

Nine years ago, when I first came here, there were several small wooden shops in front of this wall. Some of the prisoners worked in those shops as carpenters, engravers, woodworkers, and jewelers. With the help of some outside middlemen who were paid commissions they sold their crafts to passengers from ships visiting the harbor. Using a little money sent to us from home, a friend of mine—who was convicted with me for the same crime—and I began working in one of those shops. Because we were quiet and well behaved, our supervisor protected us, and in return, we gave him a small part of our profit. But neither this work nor the little money we earned made us forget the outside. Think about it! We were both just 22 years old.

Outside, we were not bad lads. When we were arrested after an incident involving a prostitute and were sent to prison, we never imagined we would stay here longer than a few days. But after our trial ended and we were each sentenced to 15 years, we came to our senses. Or, more like it, we lost our senses! But what could we do? We got stuck behind these four walls. We consoled ourselves, hoping that there would be some sort of a pardon. Who serves a full-term anyway?

One day we were boiling glue in a pot in one corner of the shop. When I added a piece of wood to the fire under the pot, it accidentally whacked the wall behind it. I noticed that the stone on the wall, behind the pot where the wood hit, appeared loose. I immediately moved the fire and the pot away and, without even waiting for the stone to cool off, I began pulling it off. First, a little lime fell off. Then, a stone the size of a baking pan came off and fell on the floor. A hole appeared where the stone had been. When I bent and looked inside, I could not believe what I was seeing! A faint light was visible in the distance, at the other end of what looked like a very narrow tunnel. I immediately called my friend. He lay on the ground and looked through the hole too. "It is probably not very difficult to escape through this hole. We must escape right away," he said.

I suggested that we first "think," before rushing ahead to escape. We could not afford to do anything stupid. We put the stone back in its place and decided to wait until evening. After that, we became totally restless and could not work for the rest of that day. We kept wandering in and out of the shop.

Occasionally, when there was a lot of work to do, we gave a little money to the guard on duty that day, and in exchange, he let us stay in the shop and work overnight. On such evenings, when the guards conducted a roll call of inmates back in prison, our guard recorded us as "present." That afternoon, when the whistle blew and everyone started to go back to their cells, we gave 25 nickels and a little heroin from our secret stash to the Arab guard who was on duty that day. He joked with us saying, "You two will leave the prison as bankers!" and left. We spent the next few hours in the shop, pretending to be making men's clogs out of nutwood, decorated with mother of pearl, and waited until it became completely dark.

Then, I moved the store's lamp to a corner and removed the loose stone in front of the hole. My friend was on the lookout for the night guard. That heathen Arab guard always fell asleep in a corner after taking the heroin we gave him, but that night, he was wandering around. I slipped through the hole, which was low, close to the ground, and very narrow. My eyes were on the light at the other end of the tunnel. That evening there was no moonlight, and the other end of the tunnel was shining like a lantern that spread dark green light. I crawled a little more. My back was touching the stones above and pieces of lime were falling on the back of my neck.

After progressing forward about the height of two men, I was suddenly relieved to find I had moved into a much wider area, and pushed myself up with the help of my hands.

I was in a chamber about three feet wide and three feet long, which allowed me to stand up by slightly lowering my head. Exhausted by the crawling, and breathing heavily, I leaned against the wall beside me. While resting there, I heard a noise from the direction of the store, and the opening on that side became dark. Initially, I was scared, but then realized my friend was crawling toward me. Although we were now deep in the wall, I whispered, "Did the Arab guard fall asleep?"

As my friend crept closer to me, he responded, "He must have. It has been half an hour since I last saw him." My friend was having a harder time crawling, but eventually made it to where I was. "What kind of place is this?" he asked. "It's so wet everywhere."

It was dark and I had to search for him with my hands. When I found him, my fingers touched a leather pouch. Then I understood why he was having a harder time crawling. During the day, we had found that pouch and hid two days' worth of rations in it for both of us. We were probably not going to see anyone for a day or two. So, we had to be prepared...

I had completely forgotten about that. But my friend had not forgotten and had brought the pouch with him. I waited until my friend had rested a little, then we resumed crawling toward the other end of the tunnel. A little later, after getting close to the end, my friend suddenly stopped. Fearing that the guard on duty on top of the tower above might hear us, he crawled backwards and came to where I was. He whispered, "We cannot pass through! There is a stone blocking the way and it is impossible to proceed without removing it. The rest of the way seems okay."

I crawled with difficulty back to the store. Once there, I listened carefully to sounds from the garden. I couldn't hear any footsteps or the Arab guard's usual cough. I opened the lamp a little more. From a trunk in which we kept our work tools, I picked up a chisel and a hammer and returned to the hole.

Taking turns, we went into the tunnel and worked to remove that stone blocking our way. Afraid of making a noise, we did not use the hammer at all, but relied on the chisel to remove the mortar around the stone and loosen it. We were less than a foot away from the end of the tunnel, the tunnel which could take us to freedom. I kept saying "If only this stone would move!"

By then, my eyes had gotten used to the dark and I was able to discern objects on the outside. In front of me were the stones covering the outer rampart. However, those walls were in ruins and it was easy to get though them. Even the town's young shepherds brought their flocks there and let them graze. It was only after this incident that all the outer walls were repaired.

That night, each of us went in and out of the tunnel four times, tirelessly working to remove the stone blocking us. I was the last one in. After working for half an hour, the stone began rolling in front of me along with a lot of plaster. I was ecstatic! My friend, hearing the noise inside, was becoming increasingly impatient. I grabbed the stone tightly with both hands and began to roll it backwards until I was back in the shop. As soon as I got it out, I pushed the stone into a corner and immediately returned to the hole.

While trying to remove the stone, I had not looked outside. When I got close to the end and finally looked outside, I saw that dawn had already broken. I stuck my head out slightly and saw the shadow of a guard who was on duty on top of a tower only 50 feet away.

I was drenched in sweat. I slowly began to return to the store. My friend was anxiously waiting for me in the area with the wider chamber.

"It's a shame, we cannot escape!" I said.

At first, my friend laughed. Then, he began crawling toward the end of the hole. However, a little later he too came back. We stood next to one another. By then, it was light enough to see each other's faces.

"This night is over, hopefully another night!" I said.

Nevertheless, after getting so close, and briefly sticking my head out to freedom, I found it hard to go back. My friend shook his head and said, "There is no other night; we must escape tonight."

"There is no 'tonight;' it has passed. You must speak of 'today.'"

"All right; we must escape today," my friend replied.

At first, I too did not want to go back. But while trying to convince my friend, I ended up persuading myself, not him. In the end, I was so convinced and so fearful that I screamed, "If you want, you can go; I will stay. I have no desire to be killed by a gendarmerie bullet!"

As I began to crawl toward the store, my friend pleaded behind me, "Don't go buddy! We can surely fool the guards. Before it gets completely light, we can escape by moving slowly and hiding in the bushes, if necessary."

However, my heart was pumping very fast as I feared for my life, so I continued crawling in the direction of the store. In my haste, my clothes got torn to shreds. Eventually, I got back to the store and put the original stone we had removed back in its place. Then, I waited for the morning and for the cells to open.

That day, at mid-morning, our attempted escape came to light. The guards and gendarmeries quickly filled the store. By then, partly from fear and partly from confusion, I had almost turned into a fool. They moved the loose stone and the tunnel behind it was exposed. When they looked through, the other end of the tunnel was clearly visible, and now it looked rather large. The path to the other end was unobstructed. One of the gendarmeries drew his rifle and fired swiftly, twice. We heard the bullets hit the outer rampart ahead. The guards emptied all the stores immediately and began inspecting all the walls. The tunnel from where my friend had escaped was quickly repaired by tightly sealing both its ends. Since then, operating such stores has been forbidden.

They didn't beat me much. Because I did not escape, the prison manager, the police chief, and the public prosecutor all felt sorry for me and took pity on me. But I wish they had beaten me to death!

For a while, the gray-haired prisoner kept quiet. It was as if his half-closed eyes were chasing a dream. Then, without turning his head to me, he lamented:

Damn it! I was stupid, so stupid! Is a gendarmerie bullet worse than 15 years in prison? Because of fear, I wasted my youth!

Whereas him.... who knows where he is? He was never seen around here again. Perhaps he moved to another country and settled among people who don't know him. He is probably behaving himself. Who knows, maybe he has a family; a wife, children. If I wanted, I could have been with him. But, that one moment's fear... That damn fear!

The gray-haired man's chin muscles tightened. I had never seen anyone so angry and so disgusted with himself. This self-hatred must have been piling up day after day, and it became such a deep grudge that it was as if he was spitting it out and throwing it at his own cowardice.

The workers across the way had lowered the wall quite a bit. We both got up and walked in that direction. Suddenly, we heard the noise of rolling stones. The workers stepped back. Trying not to laugh, the gray-haired prisoner remarked, "They must have come to that wider, empty chamber I was telling you about, right in the middle of the wall. Since that time, I have been wondering why it was constructed, for what purpose, but I could never figure it out. Who knows? Once upon a time, were there passages and doors within these walls?"

The workers went near a hole which was exposed after those stones rolled off and they began looking inside. They were manually moving a few more stones to the side, when suddenly, a look of horror crossed their faces. They rose.

Everyone nearby, including the grey-haired prisoner and I, walked in that direction. By now, the workers had reduced the wall down to just one meter high. We climbed it and went near the hole. Everyone there was standing in a circle and looking down. We got close and looked down as well...

Just then, I felt someone grabbing my hand and squeezing it tightly. His hand was shaking. Lying there, on top of moss-covered stones that had probably not seen sunlight for thousands of years, was a white human skeleton!

Most of the bones had separated from one another. Near the feet was a pair of old shoes, and a little further, a leather pouch. I lifted my head and looked at the grey-haired prisoner next to me. He was still squeezing my hand and trembling.

His face was very pale, and expressed utter disbelief. It was the look of someone who had just narrowly escaped death and who was embracing life...

Duvar

Uzun zamanlar deniz kenarında ve surlar içindeki bir hapishanede kaldım. Kalın duvarlara vuran suların sesi taş odalarda çınlar ve uzak yolculuklara çağırırdı.

Tüylerinden sular damlayarak surların arkasından yükseliveren deniz kuşları demir parmaklıklara hayretle gözlerini kırparak bakarlar ve hemen uzaklaşırlardı.

Bir mahpusu dünya ile hiç alakası olmayan bir zindana kapamak ona en büyük iyiliği yapmaktır. Onu en çok yere vuran şey, hürriyetin elle tutulacak kadar yakınında bulunmak, aynı zamanda ondan ne kadar uzak olduğunu bilmektir. On adım ötede en büyük hürriyetlere götüren denizi dinlemek ve sonra aradaki kalın kale duvarlarına gözleri dikerek bakmaya, denizi yalnız muhayyilede görmeye mecbur kalmak az azap mıdır? Bahçede insanın ayakucuna inerek ekmek kırıntılarını toplayan ve aynı hürriyetsiz topraklarda sağa sola adım atan bir kuşun bir kanat vuruşuyla bu duvarları aşarak serbestliklerle kucaklaşmaya gittiğini görmektense, nefes almaktan başka hürriyeti hatırlatacak hiçbir şey bulunmayan bir yerde kapanmak daha iyi değil midir?

Fakat benim kaldığım hapishanede her şey, her ses, hürriyeti gözlerin önüne kadar getirmek, sonra birdenbire çekip götürmek için yapılmış gibiydi. Surların üstünde büyüyen ufak ağaçlar, yosunlu taşlardan aşağı sarkan sarı çiçekler bir bahar havası içinde eli kolu bağlı olmanın bütün acılarını içime dökerdi. Uçsuz bucaksız gökte bir kuğu gibi ağır ağır yüzen küçük beyaz bulutlar benden bir tek teselliyi: unutmayı alırlardı. Ve burada konuşulan şeyler hep eskiye, dışarıya ait şeylerdi.

Sanki hiç kimse buraya girdikten sonra yaşamıyor yahut hafızası bunu zapt etmiyordu. Buradaki hayattan bahsetmek lazım gelince de o kadar isteksiz anlatılırdı ki, insanda, söyleyene azap veren bu şeyleri susturmak arzusu uyanırdı.

Yalnız kır saçlı bir mahpus bana hapishaneye ilk geldiği senelere ait bir vaka anlattı. Belki bunu ona sıkılmadan anlattıran, içeriden ziyade dışarıya ait olmasıydı. Bu, yarı kalmış bir firar hikâyesiydi.

Yalnız daha evvel hapishanenin duvarlarından bahsedelim:

Avlunun dört tarafını çeviren surlar kara tarafında kalın ve birbiri arkasına birkaç tane idiler. Bir zamanlar burası şehrin iç sarayı imiş ve şimdi sarı yüzlü, sakallı ve dünyadan uzak zavallıların dolaştığı bu bahçede asırlarca önce genç cariyeler, belki aynı hürriyet aşkıyla gözlerini yukarı çevirip denizi dinleyerek, dolaşırlarmış. Bu kalın surlar onları hem yabancı gözlerden, hem de düşmandan korumak için yapılmış.

Şimdi yer yer çöken ve üzerlerinde biten bin türlü ot altında taşları görünmez olan bu duvarların garp köşesindeki kısmının yıktırılmasına başlanmıştı. Buraya yeni münferit (hapishanede tek kişilik hücre) daireler yaptırılacağı söyleniyordu.

Bir gün yukarıda söylediğim kır saçlı mahpusla birlikte bu yıktırılan duvarı seyrediyor, kazmayı vurdukça parça parça aşağı dökülen harçlara bakıyorduk. Sekiz metre kadar geniş olan surun yıktırılması epey uzun sürüyordu ve dış bahçenin bu tarafına gelmelerine müsaade olunan emniyetli yahut eski mahpuslar, uzun seneler içinde pek bol olarak görülmeyen bu "eğlenceyi" sabahtan akşama kadar oturup seyrediyorlardı.

Duvar yarı yarıya yıkılmıştı ki, benim yanımda sesini çıkarmadan duran kır saçlı mahpus yavaşça kulağıma eğildi:

"Bir zamanlar ben bu duvardan kaçacaktım!" dedi.

Merakla yüzüne baktım. O, bahçenin bir kenarındaki kuru ayva ağacına doğru yürüdü. Yan yana çömeldik, gözlerini parça parça aşağı düşen duvardan ayırmadan anlattı:

"Dokuz sene evvel, yeni hapse düştüğümün birinci senesinde bu duvarların dibinde ahşap dükkânlar vardı. Bazı mahpuslar orada marangozluk, oymacılık, kuyumculuk yapar ve çıkardıkları işleri dışarıdaki komisyonculara vererek limana gelen vapurlarda sattırırlardı. Biz de, cürüm arkadaşımla birlikte, evimizden beş on kuruş getirterek şu şimdi yıkılan duvarın önündeki bir dükkânda çalışmaya başladık. Sessiz insanlar olduğumuz için müdür bizi koruyordu. Biz de karımızdan ona üç beş kuruş ayırıyorduk. Fakat ne bu iş, ne de kazanç bize dışarısını unutturamıyordu. Düşün! İkimiz de yirmi iki yaşındaydık.

Dışarıda ele avuca sığar şey değildik. Bir orospu kadın yüzünden vukuat yapıp içeri düştüğümüz zaman, burada birkaç günden fazla kalacağımızı aklımız kesmiyordu. Fakat cezamız tasdik olup on beş sene yüklendikten sonra aklımız başımıza geldi. Daha doğrusu aklımız başımızdan gitti. Ama ne yaparsın? Dört taraf dört duvar. Belki af çıkar; cezasını sonuna kadar yatan kaç kişi var ki? diye kendimizi avutmaya çalıştık.

Bir gün dükkânın bir köşesinde tutkal kaynatıyorduk. Çanağın altına sürdüğüm odun, duvarın taşına çarptı. Bana, taş yerinden oynar gibi geldi. Hemen ateşi ve çanağı oradan kaldırdım, taşın soğumasını beklemeden yapıştım. Azıcık kireç döküldükten sonra, koca bir tepsi ekmeği kadar büyük olan taş yere düştü. Eğilerek içeri baktım. Gözlerime inanamayacaktım: Uzakta, ta ileride dar bir ışık görünüyordu. Hemen arkadaşımı çağırdım. O da yere yatarak bakmaya başladı. Sonra bana dönüp:

"Bu delikten dışarı çıkmak zor olmasa gerek, hemen kaçalım!" dedi.

Ben kendisine "düşünelim" diye cevap verdim. Acemilik etmeye gelmezdi. Akşama kadar iş göremedik, bir içeri, bir dışarı dolaştık.

Bazı geceler, iş çok olursa, gardiyana beş on kuruş vererek dükkânda kalmak mümkündü. Gardiyan, koğuş yoklamasında bizi mevcut gösterirdi. O akşam düdük çalıp herkes koğuşlarına giderken Arap gardiyanın eline bir yirmi beş kuruşlukla bir tutam esrar sıkıştırdık. O da: "Hapishaneden banker olup çıkacaksınız ellâlem!" diye yarenlik ederek gitti. Gece oluncaya kadar ceviz takozlarını keserle yontup sözüm ona sedefli nalın yaparak vakit geçirdik.

Yatsıdan sonra lambayı köşeye çekerek taşı oradan aldım, arkadaş pencereden nöbetçi gardiyanı gözlüyordu. Kâfir Arap her sefer esrarı çekince bir köşede uyur kalırdı ama bu sefer domuzuna dolaşacağı tutmuştu. Ben delikten içeri süzüldüm.

Gözüm öbür baştaki delikteydi. Ay ışığı olmadığı için orası şimdi koyu yeşil bir fener gibi parlıyordu. Biraz daha sürünerek ilerledim. Sırtım taşlara dokunuyor, enseme kireçler dökülüyordu.

İki adam boyu kadar gittikten sonra birden ferahladım.

Elimle iki yanımı, üstümü yoklayınca geniş bir yerde olduğumu anladım, yine yoklaya yoklaya doğruldum.

Burası üç adım eninde, üç adım boyunda bir yerdi. Başımı eğerek ayakta durabiliyordum. Duvara dayanarak solumaya başladım. Sürünürken oldukça yorulmuştum. Böylece biraz bekledikten sonra dükkân tarafında bir patırtı oldu ve delik karardı. Önce korktum, sonra baktım bizim oğlan geliyor. Sanki bu yerin dibindeki delikte bizi duyacaklarmış gibi, yavaş sesle:

"Arap gardiyan uyudu mu ki?" diye sordum. Yattığı yerde ilerlemeye çalışarak: "Öyle olmalı, yarım saatten beri dolaşmaz oldu!" dedi. O benden daha zor sürünebiliyordu. Nihayet benim durduğum yere geldi, hemen:

"Burası ne biçim yer? diye sordu. Sonra ellerini duvarda gezdirerek söylendi:

"Vıyy, her yanlar da yaş!"

Elimle onu aradım, parmaklarıma meşin bir torba dokundu.

O zaman ne diye zor zoruna sürüklenebildiğini anladım.

Gündüzün acele ile bu torbayı bulmuş, belli etmemek için yalnız kendi tayınlarımızı içine koyarak saklamıştık. Belki bir gün, iki gün insan yüzü göremeyecektik...

Ben bunu unutmuştum bile, arkadaş unutmamış ve beraber

getirmiş. O da biraz dinlendikten sonra: "Haydi bakalım dayan!" dedim. Bu sefer o öne düşerek şimdi daha yakına gelen deliğe doğru ilerlemeye başladı. Ben de yere uzanarak arkasından gitmeye hazırlandım. Önümdeki, birdenbire durdu: "Buradan geçilmez!" dedi. Başı deliğe yaklaştığı için, dışarıda, kalenin üstünde dolaşan candarmanın duymasından korkuyor ve yavaş konuşuyorduk. Sonra, sesi taşların ve kendi elbiselerinin arasında boğulmaktaydı. Ben kalktım; o geri geri sürünerek geldi.

"Delik birdenbire darlaştı. Bir taş var, onu söktürmek lazım. Ondan sonrası yine ferah!" dedi.

O sıkıntılı yolu bir daha geçerek dükkâna döndüm. Bahçeyi bir güzel dinledim: Ne ayak sesi, ne de Arap'ın öksürüğü duyulmuyordu. Lambayı biraz açtım. Sandığın içinden bir keski ile bir çekiç alarak geri döndüm.

Ondan sonra sıra ile deliğe girip çalışmaya başladık. Ses çıkarmamak için çekici hiç kullanmıyor, yalnız keski ile taşın etrafındaki harçları dökmeye, taşı oynatmaya çabalıyorduk. Bizi dışarı atacak olan deliğe yarım adım bile yoktu. "Bir şu taş düşse!" diyordum.

Gözüm karanlığa alıştığı için dışarısını seçebiliyordum.

Karşımda öteki surun taşları vardı. Fakat bu surlar pek harap olduğu için aralarından geçmek kolaydı. Kasabadaki oğlanlar bile kuzularını alıp burada yayarlardı. Bu vakadan sonra hepsini tamir ettirdiler.

Böylece her birimiz üç dört kere girip çıktık. En son ben girmiştim. Yarım saat kadar uğraştıktan sonra taş, bir sürü sıva ile beraber, önüme yuvarlanıverdi. Sevincimden deli gibi oldum. Arkada sesleri duyan arkadaşım da sabırsızlanıyordu. Ellerimle sımsıkı sarılarak taşı geri geri getirdim. Onu bir kenara iter itmez deliğe doğru atıldım.

Fakat ben bu işle uğraşırken hiç dışarı doğru göz atmamıştım;

deliğe yaklaşınca ne bakayım: Şafak sökmüş bile.

Başımı yavaşça uzattım ve elli adım kadar ötedeki kalede nöbetçi candarmanın gölgesini gördüm.

Tere gömülüvermiştim. Ağır ağır geriye döndüm ve:

"Yazık, kaçamayız!" dedim.

Arkadaşım evvela güldü ve deliğe kendisi girdi. Fakat biraz sonra o da geldi. Karşı karşıya durduk, artık gözlerimiz birbirimizi seçiyordu.

"Bu akşam geçti, başka bir akşam inşallah!" dedim.

Fakat bu kadar yaklaştıktan, hatta serbestliğin içine böyle başını uzatıp baktıktan sonra insana geri dönmek pek zor geliyor.

Arkadaş başını salladı:

"Başka akşamı falan yok, bu akşam gideriz!" dedi.

"Artık bu akşam kalmadı, bugün diye konuş!"

"Peki, bugün gideriz!"

İlkönce ben de geri dönmeyi ister değildim, fakat bunun lazım olduğunu ona anlatırken onu değil kendimi kandırdım.

En sonunda sözlerime o kadar inanmış ve kendimi o kadar korkutmuştum ki: "Sen istersen git, ben kalırım, candarma kurşunuyla geberecek halim yok!" diye bağırdım, hızla geriye dönüp dükkâna doğru sürünmeye başladım. O arkamdan bağırdı:

"Ülen gitme! Candarmanın gözünü avlar, daha ortalık adamakıllı aydınlanmadan otların arasına sine sine gideriz!" dedi.

Fakat benim yüreğim, kör olası bir korku, bir can korkusu ile öyle yaman atmaya başlamıştı ki, üstümü başımı yırta yırta kendimi dükkâna zor fırlattım ve taşı eski yerine kapatarak sabahı ve koğuşların açılmasını bekledim.

O gün kuşluk vakti iş meydana çıktı. Gardiyanlar, candarmalar dükkâna doluverdiler. Ben yarı korkudan, yarı şaşkınlıktan aptala dönmüştüm. Taşı çektiler, delik meydana çıktı. Eğilip bakınca öbür baştaki delik, bu sefer kocaman olarak görünüyordu.

Yol bomboştu... Bir candarma mavzerini uzatarak iki sıkı attı. Kurşunların karşı surlara vurdukları duyuldu. Hemen bütün dükkânları boşalttılar. Duvarlar muayene edildi, bizim arkadaşın kaçtığı delik iki yandan ördürüldü ve bir daha böyle dükkân açmak falan yasak edildi.

Ben çok dayak yemedim. Kendim kaçmadığım için hapishane müdürü, karakol kumandanı, hatta müddeiumumi halime acıdılar. Fakat keşke dayaktan öldürselerdi!"

Kır saçlı mahpus bir müddet sustu. Yarı kapalı gözleri bir hayali kovalıyor gibiydi. Başını bana çevirmeden, küfrediyormuş gibi keskin keskin:

"Ah... ne enayilik ettim!" dedi, "Ne enayilik ettim! Bir candarma kurşunu on beş seneden daha mı kötü sanki? Bir korku yüzünden gençliğimi yok ettim."

"Hâlbuki o... kim bilir şimdi nerelerdedir? Bir daha buralarda görünmedi. Herhalde uzak bir memlekette, kendisini tanımayanlar arasında yerleşti, akıllı uslu adam oldu... Belki çoluk çocuğa da karışmıştır. İstesem ben de onunla beraber olabilirdim. Fakat bir dakikalık korku... O kahrolası korku..."

Çenesinin adaleleri gerilmişti. Hayatımda kendisini bu kadar istihkar eden, kendisine bu kadar kızan insan görmedim; her gün üst üste yığılarak müthiş bir kin halini alan bu nefret dudaklarından çıkarak bir tükürük halinde kendi korkaklığının yüzüne fırlatılıyordu.

Karşıda ameleler duvarı iyice alçaltmışlardı, ikimiz de ayağa kalkarak o tarafa yürüdük. Tam bu sırada gürültüyle birkaç taşın yuvarlandığı duyuldu.

Ameleler geri fırladılar. Yanımdaki gülümsemeye çalışarak:

"O benim söylediğim boşluğa geldiler galiba, duvarın tam orta yerindeki boşluğa... Ben o zamandan beri çok düşündüm, ama bunun ne diye yapıldığını bulamadım. Kim bilir, eski zamanlarda burada duvar içinde yollar, kapılar mı vardı?" dedi.

Ameleler bu sefer taşların düştüğü deliğe yaklaşmışlar, içeri doğru bakıyorlardı. Birkaç taşı daha ellerine alıp bir kenara koyduktan sonra birdenbire, yüzlerinde elle tutulabilecek bir dehşet ifadesiyle, doğruldular...

Etrafta bulunanlar ve bunların arasında kır saçlı mahpusla ben, o tarafa yürüdük; artık bir metreye kadar inmiş olan duvara tırmanarak deliğe yaklaştık. Herkes halka olmuş, ses çıkarmadan, aşağı bakıyordu. Bunları aralayarak biz de sokulduk ve gözlerimizi oraya çevirdik...

Elime birisinin yapıştığını, sımsıkı tuttuğunu ve sinirli sinirli titrediğini hissettim.

Orada, binlerce seneden beri güneş görmemiş olan rutubetli taşların üstünde bembeyaz bir insan iskeleti uzanıyordu.

Çoğu birbirinden ayrılmış olan kemiklerin ayak ucunda bir çift eski kundura, yanı başında meşin bir torba vardı.

Başımı kaldırarak yanımdakine baktım. O hala elimi tutuyor ve sinirli sinirli sıkmakta devam ediyordu.

Yüzü sapsarıydı ve bu yüzde, henüz ölümden kurtulanlarda görülen şaşkın bir hayata sarılış vardı...

Escape

Toni Margarita Plummer

Ivan was the one who put the thought into her head. She would have been happy right now, carefree. Not hoping to see a red splotch each time she pulled down her underwear, not wasting pads in useless anticipation. Not dreading the worst conversation of her life with her parents. He'd never put his dick in her, but he *had* put in the thought.

"I think I might be pregnant," Micaela finally told her best friend Elena during lunch time. They were sitting up against the lockers outside the biology classroom. Someone's padlock dug into Micaela's shoulder, and the heat from the hard concrete penetrated her polyester plaid skirt.

"I thought you were a virgin," Elena said, rummaging through her chili cheese fries with lilac nails the length of a sloth's.

"I know!" Micaela shrieked. "That's what's so messed up about it."

Elena stopped chewing. "Wait, what?"

"Okay, so that guy I mentioned—" Micaela lowered her voice, even though of course Ivan didn't go to their school. "We've been messing around, right? But we've never actually done it. And then last week, he asks me, 'What if some of my soldiers got past the gate?'"

"The gate?"

"It's a figure of speech." Her eyes dipped low. "The gate."

"That's really unlikely, isn't it?" Elena asked. "And doesn't a gate swing out? Or in, I guess."

Micaela shook her head. "Listen, he asked if I'd had my period lately. And I haven't."

Elena held a loaded fry over her open mouth. "When's the last time you had it?"

"I don't know, I don't keep track! Do you remember when it was I borrowed that tampon from you?"

"Hm…" Elena chewed.

"It was after gym."

Micaela remembered the tampon with some annoyance. It hadn't been the kind with the plastic applicator that she normally used. Elena only had one of those small, hard bullets of cotton that she had to push in with the tip of her finger. It had made her late, trying to get the thing in deep enough so that it didn't feel like she was walking around with a bat between her legs.

"Was that the day Jackie got caught stuffing her bra?" Elena asked.

"That happened like a month ago!"

"That was hilarious." Elena shook her head and excavated another fry. "Yeah, I don't know."

Micaela lie on her bed, her body tense, the springs from the old mattress jabbing into her back. It bothered her. Well, the whole thing bothered her, of course. But the expression Ivan had used. Soldiers getting past the gate. He had never warned her that could happen. And who said they could do that? Who gave them permission? She envisioned little sperm wearing helmets, throwing hand grenades, making a mess! And what could she do but wait? Maybe another expression would make her feel better. She wracked her brain but could not think of one that would ease her anxiety. Finally she got up to get a drink.

Her brother, Alex, and older cousins were in the living room watching an old *Star Wars* movie. The characters were in a desert and

Harrison Ford knocked the guy in a helmet with some pole by mistake, and the guy's jetpack went off and he flew, crashed into the side of a ship, and tumbled down into the sand where he rolled into the mouth of some kind of giant, toothy creature.

"What's that thing in the sand?" Micaela asked.

"The Sarlacc," Alex said.

"What does it do?"

He shrugged. "It eats you."

Her cousin Paco imitated a British accent, "And digests you over a thousand years."

Micaela frowned. "Wouldn't you be dead long before then?"

"That's not really the point."

"Well, what is the point?"

"That it fucking hurts!" Alex said.

Micaela rolled her eyes. She watched the Sarlacc grab a man with its tentacle and try to pull him into its gaping mouth.

"What are you staring at?" Paco asked.

"Maybe it's just misunderstood."

"You know *Star Wars*?" Micaela asked Elena the next day at school.

"Uh huh." Elena opened her can of Sprite with one mauve nail and gulped.

"You know that sand creature on Tatooine? Jabba the Hutt wants to feed Luke Skywalker to it?"

"What?"

"When Leia is wearing the bikini."

"Oh, yeah."

"Maybe it's more like that."

"Maybe what's more like that?"

"My vagina."

Elena choked on her soda.

"Maybe that's what happened. Although, then it seems like it's a monster. Like it wanted to eat up stuff. That's kinda gross, right? And not true! Unless it has a mind of its own…"

Elena coughed. "Can we talk about something else please?"

"Elena!" Micaela put her head in her hands. "When am I gonna get my freaking period?"

"Don't worry, it'll come. You're a virgin, right?"

"Yes," she said through gritted teeth. "I am a virgin."

Elena tipped her can toward her mouth, then slowed and narrowed her eyes. "Are you sure?"

Micaela had always considered herself a virgin. But if she was afraid she might be pregnant, was she *really* a virgin? All this time she had thought she was holding something back from Ivan. Had she been lying to herself?

He had tried to talk her into having sex a bunch of times. He would be gentle. He'd wear a condom. He felt super strongly about her. But she had always been firm in her refusal. He stopped asking and instead moved his penis along her, outside. She let him do it. But if he got too near the center or if his dick felt too hard on her soft spots, she'd complain, "You're poking me!"

Was a virgin someone who'd been poked? She Googled it.

"Virgin: A person who has never had intercourse." That was right, she never had. Oral yes, but did that count? You couldn't get pregnant that way. She recalled Health class, where they did call it sex.

Second definition: "a person who is naïve, innocent, or inexperienced in a certain context." Was she naïve? Was she innocent? She was not innocent like she used to be when she was a little girl maybe. But did that make her guilty?

For adjective, the entry read, "not yet touched, used or exploited, e.g. virgin forests." Well, she *had* been touched. Quite a lot. Had she been used or exploited? She hadn't thought so, but maybe. She was pretty sure she could not call herself a virgin forest anymore. Ivan had set foot in her, stepped on her twigs.

What had they said about the Virgin Mary? That she didn't "know" man. What did that mean? Did Micaela *know* Ivan? She certainly knew things about him. She knew what his penis looked like, and how it felt. She knew he liked to bite her, on the arm, on the thigh. But that kind of knowing seemed very fuzzy, not helpful.

Micaela looked online for things she could know.

Friday night, as usual, Micaela and Elena sat in the back row of the church cafeteria exchanging notes beneath their hard, metal chairs. This week a married woman had come to speak to their youth group.

"And that is why each morning I show my outfit to my husband before I leave for work, to make sure I'm not showing too much skin and that I am dressed modestly." The woman looked around the room, especially at the girls, Micaela thought, perhaps to see if her wisdom had sunk in. "Does anyone have any questions?"

Micaela's hand shot up, while with the other she passed a reply to Elena that read, "Honey, am I showing too much vulva?" "I have a question about Mary."

The woman smiled. "Our Blessed Virgin Mary. Go ahead."

"Was Mary *really* a virgin?" she asked, ignoring Elena's muffled laughter beside her. "I mean, isn't it true that the word 'young' was mistranslated into 'virgin' when the text was translated from Hebrew to Greek?"

The woman looked exactly as if someone had paused her with a remote.

"And that's all we have time for." Ivan walked over from the side of the room, stuffing his cell phone into his back pocket. "Thank you so much for coming," he said to the woman. "Micaela, stay after class. We need to talk." He walked the woman out, lamenting, "These kids."

After class, Micaela and Ivan did not talk. They did what they always did, make out in Ivan's car behind the community center.

He was giving her an enormous hickey she would have to cover with foundation, maybe even a turtleneck, and it was April. Also, she didn't own a turtleneck.

Since his "soldiers/gate" comment, he had not ventured below her waist. Micaela was not sure whether to feel relieved or insulted. "Have you had your period yet?" he asked when he came up for air.

She shook her head no.

He sighed. "If it doesn't come by Monday, we're gonna have to do a pregnancy test."

Micaela pulled away from him and pressed back into the car seat. "A pregnancy test? I don't wanna do that."

"Micaela, it's gotta be done. We have to be responsible."

He didn't even blink when he said this.

Monday night they were on the quest. They had told her mom they were going to Adoration at a neighboring parish. Instead they drove to a CVS a few cities away. Ivan walked quickly, scanning each aisle, and Micaela followed, her sweatshirt dangling from her head by its hood, the sleeves hanging limp. At the feminine products section, they were greeted with an array of maxi pads, tampons, and pregnancy tests. Ivan began reading boxes. Micaela spun in place, making squeaky sounds on the floor with her shoes.

"It's probably not the best marketing idea," she said, "to have the pregnancy tests right by the condoms."

He didn't respond.

"Oh, look at these ones." She picked up a box of condoms. "They're 'almost as if you're wearing nothing at all.' Do you remember that Simpsons episode? With Flanders and his new ski suit? 'Why it feels like I'm wearing nothing at all, nothing at all...' and his butt just keeps wiggling in Homer's mind?"

He still did not respond.

"'Stupid sexy Flanders.'"

"Micaela," Ivan said, his eyes closed like when they all held hands and stood in a circle to pray, Micaela spying with one eye open. "I am...I am this close to losing it."

She turned away from him and spread her legs to balance on the sides of her feet. He was angry with her. For what?

For not *really* being a virgin? For just being young?

"I thought that was you!"

Micaela turned to see a woman smiling madly at Ivan, her shopping cart piled high with boxes of diapers.

"Erica, hi," Ivan said, and Micaela could tell from his voice this was not good.

"I never see you in here! What brings you to the neighborhood?" The woman's eyes were wide with wonder, as if Ivan appearing in her CVS was some kind of blessed event.

Ivan struggled to answer, and the woman's eyes slid to Micaela. Micaela realized too late that she shouldn't have been watching them. She should have pretended not to know him.

"Hi," the woman said uncertainly.

"Hi!" Micaela nearly shouted. She was standing in front of the lubricants and she grabbed a box. "Here's what I wanted. Silky. My favorite." And she ran out of the aisle, her sweatshirt slipping off behind her.

Some minutes later, Micaela saw Ivan approach the check-out counters. He didn't look at her when she went to stand behind him, just placed a few pregnancy tests and some other random stuff on the conveyor belt. He had her sweatshirt tucked under his arm.

It was cold with the air-conditioning, but after her screw-up with the woman, she didn't dare to ask him for her sweatshirt. She stood still, hugging her goose-pimpled arms and looking out the windows. The silence was awkward, but it was also a magnet, and as much as she wanted to go off on her own, she could not move. They'd come in together, and they would leave together. And when they got to his apartment, she'd have to go into his bathroom and open up one of those boxes. When would she get to leave him then? Never, maybe. At least, not really, not if she carried something of his.

Dread settled in her gut, and the feeling spread to her chest, her limbs. She felt sick. Achy at her core. And then, standing so still, she felt the slightest of movements. Something only she could have felt. A cramp!

A familiar craving jolted her to unfreeze. She snatched a chocolate bar and a soda from the mini fridge and dumped them on the belt just as the cashier was about to pick up the divider.

Ivan glared at the new items but didn't say anything. He nodded at the cashier to ring them up.

Back in the car driving home, Ivan banged the steering wheel. "Shit! Shit! I am so careful! You know I am so careful! She's gonna tell everyone. I'm fucked!"

Micaela pulled the chocolate bar out of the shopping bag and tore open the wrapper with her teeth. The cramps ebbed like waves, and she let herself be rocked. She closed her eyes, envisioned the saturation of her underwear, her jeans.

Ivan went on cursing. She let him.

Outside the car, the twilight world rolled by, one long strip of silhouettes, the sky much lighter, and wide open.

Maybe she wasn't *really* a virgin. But she was something better. Free.

The Bank of Paradise

Monique McIntosh

Truths yet to be known, that:

If the dead can indeed wake up, there's only one safe way to rouse them. Before their grave, light one (1) soft, drippy red candle. The dead will stir, sluggish, cantankerous, the scent like hands running through their sleepy scalps. Bow three times in greeting. Lay down your gifts: crispy fried pork, cups of pale tea, sliced oranges to cleanse the palate. White rum is welcomed. And of course, money—not the monies of everyday commerce, but neon-bright cash certified by the Bank of Paradise. Do not question how currency for the afterlife is produced and sold by your cousin's pharmacy down the road. Instead, be grateful that a suitcase of money from the Bank of Paradise costs less than your box-lunch. Burn said banknotes and scatter the ashes. Kneel down. Say your prayers. Beg for mercy. The ancestors may not answer you. There is always the risk that no one is listening. But the uncertainty itself holds a portion of divinity — that the dead may still find life within the crevices of your doubt.

Waltham Park, St. Andrew, Jamaica
Gah San Day, 10 April 2004
Joseph Tibbs, second generation caretaker of the Waltham Park Historical Chinese Cemetery, picks his way through the graves and

family mausoleums. A bag of oranges swings by his side. His feet move on their own, following some primal memory of early morning light, of his young feet following his father, Albert — the first generation caretaker of the Waltham Park Historical Chinese Cemetery.

Overnight, the thick brush he cleared yesterday has returned, scattering dead leaves across the gravestones. Joseph will tend to them. But first things first. He squats beside the flat cement headstone of Georgie Leung. The black wrought iron fence that surrounded Georgie's headstone is long gone, stolen for scrap metal. Joseph wipes away the fallen leaves and picks at the dirt, until inky black characters appear beneath.

"Morning," says Joseph. He takes out an orange and his father's knife, slicing through the fruit's soft navel. Exposed pulp looks up at him in perfect quarters, ready for teeth. He cuts open two more and lays them out on the concrete slab, pulpy insides facing the sky.

Joseph sighs. His father Albert told him tales of when the cemetery was awake, how nightly its occupants came scratching at the door of the caretaker's house, rattling mahjong tiles. And he beat every last one of them, Albert would boast. Albert Tibbs, best mahjong man of Waltham Park Historical Chinese Cemetery. His father said many things.

But Joseph is an old man now. He needs to call those boys from down the road to help clear the bush before family members come for Gah San, this day of the dead, the annual bargaining with the ancestors. The few descendants that still come will pick through the mud, counting headstones, wondering if their great-grandpa was buried one or two graves behind the fat stone cherub squatting over Mr. Wong from Spanish Town. And Joseph will say yes indeed, he believes so, though unfortunately there are no stone angels anymore. On cue, these descendants will stop and gaze with shock across the yard and its muddy paths and its absent grills and the absent headstones, ripped away like buds from their stems by thieves.

This is the final death, when a graveyard dies.

But not yet. For now Joseph enjoys this quiet, the chill of this mostly intact concrete slab radiating up his arm. So he does not see the muddy hump rise just two graves beyond. At first just a lump of wet earth, inching its way towards him. Then the mound of mud arches its back, raising a muddy face and a dark chasm where a mouth should be, growing wider and wider until soft breath echoes through, rustling the leaves across Georgie Leung's headstone.

"Dad," the body says, collapsing, limbs outstretched and beckoning. Joseph rushes to the body and wipes away the mud. The young bruised face of his first and only son, Donovan Tibbs, looks back at him, eyes closed, breathing shallow. One broken arm lops to one side. Mud trails behind him, and something else. Blood, thinks Joseph. Joseph scrapes away at the mud coating his one and only son's big head, which he has not seen for so long. Blood clots in a hard gash above Donovan's ear. But this is not enough to bleed out the blood congealing along a trail that runs down the end of the graveyard, where the oldest graves lie, their fine marble headstones long stolen—except the lone and miraculous, fine-veined marble of graveyard patriarch, Pa-Kung Leung.

Truths yet to be known, that:
2. The price for black market marble is now up 10 percent, as in these wet months the illicit rich find pleasure in the chill of ill-gotten marble beneath their fingertips.

3. On the 2nd of April, 1912, when Pa-Kung Leung was buried in the very first plot of this newly christened Waltham Park Chinese Cemetery, his wife May Leung and his mistress Hyacinth Tibbs stood watching on opposite sides of the grave pit. They did not look at each other. Instead

they clenched their babies tight to their chests (Georgie Leung and Alfred Tibbs, respectively). They ignored the whispers. They ignored the elders muttering why the hell did Pa-Kung wish to be buried here once and for all, with this dumb priest muttering soft words into the earth, when we should have buried him the old Hakka way? Clean and keep his bones in a clay urn, until we were ready to leave again, carrying our brood and our dead on our backs as in olden days? Because even in these modern times, no Hakka should have a home but in the wind in our ears as we seek new lands.

Instead the elders sighed, as their brethren Pa-Kung disappeared under the fine slab of Italian marble he secured before his death—white with the palest veins of pink.

Meanwhile:

4. On this same dark night, Georgie Leung's widow, "Pao Pao" Joyce Leung sits downstairs, anxious, her whole body trembling like cow foot jelly not quite set. She cracks the window. The rain slips in as she blows out her cigarette smoke through the security grill, so her son Paulie will not smell its scent. He constantly ignores her perfect logic that if said smoking has not killed her in these 87 years, then some other fate awaits her.

And besides, she tells him, it was his father Georgie who taught her to smoke so long ago, crisp in his starched Royal Air Force uniform, leaning in the doorway of the Leung family shop on Princess Street. Young Pao Pao had obliged his offer for a drag, sucking in the first wisps down her throat, ignoring the passersby eying her. It was 1945. The war was over and the whole world waited for her. And her journey could begin here, smoking in the doorway with an airman, wind still humming in his ears. This Georgie was going places. That's why she smokes, she tells Paulie—to remember the husband gone off to paradise, leaving her behind.

Pao Pao does not tell her son the truth. And good old Georgie Leung died not knowing that Pao Pao had in fact smoked her first cigarette years before, crouched on a cool headstone smoking with the best mahjong man of Waltham Park Historical Chinese Cemetery. Albert Tibbs, the boy-man who played mahjong with ghosts — a man who knew exactly where he wanted to be buried.

But never mind that. Secrets are for burying. And she's not dead yet. But still the feeling of weak-kneed jelly persists. Because somewhere in the rain waits her only grandson Michael, looking for sleep.

Unnamed bar down the road from Historical Chinese Cemetery, St. Andrew, Jamaica
Night before Gah San Day, 9 April 2004
Now let us meet Pa-Kung's great-grand baby boy Michael Leung, son of Paulie Leung, grandson of Georgie Leung, etc. This scrawny man sits in the White House Bar and Lounge off Waltham Park Road, waiting for someone to come in and kill him. He must look for someone watching him. This will be the man who will emerge from the dark to put a bullet in his head. And the bartender won't even blink, thinks Michael. He will only kiss his teeth and cuss about that Pepsi-drinking wretch who got himself shot and bled all over his nice bar.

Because nobody gives a shit about him, thinks Michael. He cannot run to anyone for help, not even to his family living in their quiet, gated townhouse complex. Although sometimes when he scores a hit uptown, he climbs over the gates and taps as quietly as he can on the glass window panes of his home, for it is the only sound in the world that makes his head not ache so.

But forget that, thinks Michael. He must keep surveillance for watchful eyes. But everybody watches him. Some staring in stark bafflement, others in sly, sideway glances at the ragged Chinese man with mad hair, sitting at the bar drinking a Pepsi Cola, because Michael has never drank alcohol a day in his life and, despite the crack coke addiction, he was not going to start now. Even though his hands shake, rattling the ice in his glass. But for now he must hide in this old bar for old men or be hunted down by his dealer for the pittance he owes him. A miniscule debt, thinks Michael. Not nearly enough to treat him so. To threaten to blow his brains out and, just for fun, to break through the lovely windowpanes of the Leung family home and crack skulls.

Michael is imagining the prospect of his dealer bashing in his Pao Pao's head, when he hears someone plop down on the barstool beside him. It is a man tall and slim like himself, but strong with the muscles of work. The grit of cement dust lingers in the crevices of his nail beds as he calls to the bartender for a Heineken. The man takes one long, deep gulp from the green bottle, oblivious to anything else. Or so he would want him to think, thinks Michael. This Heineken drinking fool thinks he can just play innocent, guzzle his beer and wait until Michael is not looking.

Michael has just about decided to slam his empty Pepsi Cola bottle on this man's head when the man comes up for air and, in the flicker of light from the TV playing the afternoon's horse races, Michael sees the soft lines of a ghost trip across the strange man's face.

He remembers in fragments. The hot white light of noon, racing each other through the old cemetery. Him igniting his father's lighter for the first time as the other boy runs the edges of the paper money (verified by the Bank of Paradise) through a razor flame. Them both watching as the fire eats away the paper, daring each other to hold on to the burning money for longer and longer and longer until they can't, until nothing is left but ashes and air.

"Donovan," says Michael to the man beside him.

Donovan Tibbs looks at the skinny man calling his name. He is about to tell this cokehead to bugger off when he sees the same flash of light: white noon, razor flame, a torch of fire and paper money burning in his hands.

"Michael?" he asks. "Shit."

They take a table in the corner of the bar, away from the old men (although the bartender watches, coyly peering through the crowd). They hunch over each other, guarding the air around them. Under the table Michael's feet quivers, tap, tap. All Michael knows, right down to his bones, to his palpitating phalanges, that Donovan will save him. Donovan Tibbs, the childhood playmate whose father and grandfather watched over the Leung family graves—the plain cement gravestone of Grandpa Georgie, and the genuine Italian marble of Pa-Kung Leung. When they were young, little Michael and little Donovan would gaze at the miraculous marble's pristine surface, dense and unscathed by nature or headstone graverobbers.

"What would they do with the marble if they got to steal it?" Little Michael had asked little Donovan.

"Anything they want," little Donovan had said. Because anything is for sale when your poor constituency has become a gang battleground. When guns were needed and real marble was precious. Especially marble like this one, with its pink veins that seemed to pulse in the flickering light of fake cash burning away, the gift withering into ash and smoke that crawled skywards to their intended recipients

"Why a dead man need money in heaven, anyways?" little Donovan had asked.

"So they don't have to beg in paradise."

"So how Black people manage?" But Donovan hadn't asked that one aloud. Instead he thought of his ancestors, those no names lurking beyond his Grandpa Alfred. Where were they buried? Who tended to their graves? Were they alone, abandoned, standing at the crossroads of eternity, washing already pristine, transcendental windshields for some petty money?

But no, that time of childhood is gone. Donovan says he is a father now. Of a little baby girl. He shows Michael a picture of the baby smiling, gummy mouth wide, eyes crinkled in laughter. And there again is the ghost, though Michael can't place it.

But the baby is so colicky, says Donovan. And though he's a mason, construction work has dried up bad.

"I wonder though," mutters Michael. "How much marble is now?" He takes another sip of his third Pepsi, hands shaking. "Italian marble."

And there again a flash of light before them both. White noon, razor flame. A bed of marble, hard white, with delicate pink vessels miraculously unbruised by time.

Truths yet to be known, that:
5. In Kingston 1911, both Mrs. Pa-Kung Leung and Hyacinth Tibbs gave birth to baby boys, Georgie Leung and Albert Tibbs respectively, precisely three months apart. They were both a respectable and identical six pounds. Before his death, Pa-Kung Leung was present at the birth of both his sons (held in separate houses, in separate constituencies of Kingston). Pa-Kung had held each son in his arms, beaming with a love unbearable at their faces, and thought, shit. They both look like me. One Black, one Chinese. But there in their sleeping faces was the ghost of him, swooping down their foreheads and eyes, curling along their cheeks and down their tiny wet mouths.

Waltham Park, St. Andrew, Jamaica
In the early hours of Gah San Day, 10 April 2004

Donavon Tibbs is not terribly sure he can smoothly extract the entire marble slab from the grave. Likely the marble is sealed tightly to its cement enclosure, protecting the body below. And since neurotic marble cracks at the slightest suggestion of electronic vibration, he will need to go old school. Perhaps scoring the edges first with a utility knife, then running a chipping hammer along the grout. A heavy wire would follow, sawing through the ancient seal. The process may take several nights working quietly in the dark, in an effort to not wake his father, Joseph Tibbs, still sleeping in the caretaker house at the end of the graveyard.

He tells Michael these facts when they arrive at the gates of the cemetery. But he is not sure Michael is listening to him. Michael nods yes, yes, of course. His whole body vibrates with affirmations. Oh shit. He's high, thinks Donovan as they both climb over the fence surrounding the cemetery. Not for the first time tonight, he thinks of turning back, going straight home to his wife and bawling baby.

They both land softly on the ground, narrowly missing a headless angel. Much of the bramble has been cleared away to the sides. He can see the tiny family mausoleums and gray markers clearly through the dark. He whispers to Michael to wait, but Michael bursts ahead, hopping over gravestones.

"Michael," calls Donovan a bit too loudly.

"What!"

"You know where you going?"

Michael stops shaking for a moment to let out a huge belly laugh that buckles his knees. He sinks to the ground.

"Don't have a clue," he whispers finally. He has lost so much weight, thinks Donovan.

"Come," he says, pulling him up. "This way." And sure enough Donovan's feet find their path, remembering the early morning march following his father Joseph and grandfather Albert to the miraculous marble headstone of Pa-Kung Leung, untouched by thieves. At night little Donovan would lie awake, waiting for the thieves to come with their hushed feet and quick hands hauling away pounds of stone and metal. Growing up in a cemetery, he knew not to believe in ghosts (tall tales at best told by Grandpa Albert). But the night thieves had frightened him – these goblins with hammers and chisels. In his childhood dreams he would see them hover over him, faceless bodies with thick hands clenching hammers, waiting for him to wake up.

So every dawn he would run to check Pa-Kung Leung's headstone, impermeable to these night goblins. And every Sunday he did his duty, scrubbing the blush marble. And little Donovan would ask Grandpa Albert, why this one? Why did this stone remain so unweathered and untouched, while others so easily got taken? And Grandpa Albert would press little Donovan's chubby fingers against the marble's tender pink veins, pink as mice's tails, and tell him that the gravestone of Pa-Kung Leung kept strong because he was waiting for us, his grandbabies and his great grandbabies to come sit with him – to scrub him clean, to feed him rum and play mahjong. And little Donovan would smile and swallow this story whole — that his mother was wrong, that they were not a long line of stupid men obsessed with a graveyard.

When they buried Albert Tibbs, only Donovan and Joseph had attended. They buried him by the caretaker's house, his body turned west to watch the cemetery's entrance. And as Donovan watched his grandfather sink into the dirt, he asked his father if Albert's stories were true. Were they related to these Leungs scattered across the graveyard? His father had shrugged. Grandpa, Joseph told him, said a lot of things. And Donovan looked out at the dying graveyard with its broken stones and bodies neglected by their own blood and thought, what the fuck? Why the hell have we stayed here so long? Where are our ancestors, the black ones, the self-evident, bare-skinned ones that need no witnesses? Don't they need a little grave scrubbing? A little pocket money for paradise? And his dad had stared at his one and only boy. And after a long silence between them he smiled and said, "a good man has many fathers."

But Donovan was sixteen then, and that wasn't nearly good enough. But somehow here he is now, his feet carrying him and Michael to the end of the graveyard, to the final resting place of Pa-Kung Leung.

"This is it then," says Michael. They both stop and watch the marble's seamless surface. Marble, says Donovan, is actually not meant to last this well outside. Granite is a better material. But somehow this stone remains impenetrable to grief.

Michael crouches down, running a finger along the lettering.

"You sure this is the one?" asks Michael.

"Yes, I'm sure."

"You know," says Michael, chucking softly. "I never learned how to read this stuff. Always skipped the class."

"It says he's from the Guangdong province. Born 1875. Has one son."

"Just the one?"

"Yeah."

"You can read this stuff?"

"I don't need to." Donovan takes out his scoring knife and paces around Michael and the grave, searching for seams. He tries not to think about those Sundays spent scrubbing and polishing the marble, how the surface shone underneath his fingers. He scrapes the knife against the cement frame.

"I can't get it out whole," he says. Michael looks up at him. His vibrations, Donovan notices, have quieted.

"What?"

"We've got to break it up and take out the pieces." He takes out his hammer and chisel.

"What? Shit. Won't it ruin it?"

"There's no way around it," says Donovan. "We can sell it off in bits."

This is what he must do. He must chip away at a low angle, let the chisel's edge scrape right through the marble, white with faint pink veins, pulsing. Are they pulsing now, these fine pink vessels, right under the surface? Warm and throbbing underneath his splayed fingers? Was that dew, or was that sweat, salty and leaking through the stone's miniscule pores?

They stand there for too long, Donovan poised over the stone, Michael standing behind him.

A fine breeze whispers over their heads, like fingers across their scalps.

"Don't do it," Michael says softly, suddenly. Surprising himself.

"No, I won't." He drops the chisel to the ground.

They do not look at each other. Instead they stand quiet, watch the marble, the elusive marks declaring the final resting place of Pa-Kung Leung, in a land so far away from his birth. Rain begins to fall, settling into the black letters.

"Hey, Chiney," says a voice behind them. They both turn around. They both promptly receive concussions as two cricket bats swing for their heads.

Just before Michael passes out, he sees the face of his attacker—that damn bartender from the White House Bar and Lounge. "I hate bartenders," thinks Michael. Further articulations of scorn fade, however, as the drug-withdrawal hum within Michael's eardrums gives way to some other rhythm, like rain on window panes, pulsing beneath the grave dirt beneath his cheek. Sleep waits for him, the kind of long, sweet sleep where food waits for you on the other side.

Just before Donovan passes out, from the corner of his eye he sees a Chinese man emerge from the dark rain, walking up behind the fugly bartender standing over him. The Chinese man wears a bush jacket of the palest blue and a straw Panama hat. He feels familiar. The man seems to smile at him, pressing his index finger over his month in the universal sign of "keep quiet while I fuck this guy over." And before Donovan loses consciousness he thinks — boy, that man looks just like me.

Truths yet to be known, that:

6. Traditionally, when news comes from a faraway land about the birth of a new boy, the Hakka elders gather, beating drums and cymbals in a riot of song seeking not melody but sheer volume, abrasive enough to penetrate Paradise, waking the ancestors and pissing them off. But who can complain for long? Not when a new child has come into the fold, new blood to keep roaming the earth.

7. Still sleepless on Gah San Day, 10th of April 2004, Pao Pao decides to cook juk porridge. And as she stands stirring the rice and water into a white blur of nothingness, she feels the roots of a laugh quivering in her cow-foot-jelly bones — a laugher of such depth she has not encountered since she buried her Georgie in 1979.

Georgie Leung had looked every inch his death, with hair that broke off in her hands as she pulled it tight. And so few had gathered for his funeral at the Waltham Park Historical Chinese Cemetery. So many of their friends had long left on those five daily flights to Miami, and off to the glossy destinations she had dreamed of as a girl. And her son Paulie was whispering I'm sorry Mum, we should have gone too. Start over again in another land. And maybe if we did, maybe, maybe.

Pao Pao had scanned those that remain: her one and only son Paulie, his young wife Rebecca and the first grandchild Michael snuggled inside her. And this old strange brown man, still tall and slim, staring so hard at her. And there again was a flash of light. Crouched on wet cement, blood-warm leg against blood-warm leg. The gossamer cloud of her first cigarette. And graveyard mahjong king Albert Tibbs who had murmured in his quiet way ImsorrymyloveImsorrysosorry. Don't make me leave here. And Pao Pao who had clenched her teeth against the smoke and the tears, thinking why the hell does this brown boy care so much about these strangers buried beneath them? Because how can piles of bones and old clothes compare to the fever of her stockingless legs against his?

And staring back at the aged face of her old lover Albert Tibbs, Pao Pao had thought shoot – am I seeing things? Is there a shadow of Georgie hanging off old Albert's face? She had kept them apart so long in her head—the man who wouldn't leave and the man who promised to go, but didn't—that she did not see their shared curvatures. Would Albert ever tell her now, after all these years, that his old lover had indeed married his half brother? And as the small crowd bowed in prayer, all Pao Pao wanted to do was laugh loud enough for the ancestors who plotted to bring her into the fold, one way or another. They were patient, waiting for the final punch line.

Yes, this same laugh from so long ago now scratches through her throat, as she stands over the stove stirring juk porridge. Despite her sleeping brood upstairs, Pao Pao knows she must let it go, let it shudder through her teeth and bounce off the pots and pans into the atmosphere, because Pao Pao suspects that the ancestors will be kind to her today. She must make her son Paulie buy more paper money, although the price will be hiked up, today of all days.

On route to Waltham Park Historical Chinese Cemetery, St. Andrew, Jamaica

Gah San Day, 10 April 2004

It is too early in the morning, and Paulie Leung is surrounded by women packed in the family van—his wife, Rebecca and his mother

Pao Pao, both chatting and sipping juk along the drive to Waltham Park Historical Chinese Cemetery. Pao Pao says he must wait until they get to the cemetery before he can eat. So they are the first to arrive, even before the reps from the Chinese Benevolent Association with the main Gah San feast of rice and whole suckling pig, skin crispy red. Paulie parks the car and gestures for his cup of juk.

"We don't have time for that Paulie," says Pao Pao. "Come." And Pao Pao is off marching through the gate, bags of paper money and paper gold bricks and paper debit cards in hand.

"Is she alright?" asks Rebecca as they follow her through the gravestones, her feet finding her way deftly through.

"Who knows?" They pass the bushes shielding their patriarch's grave. And there stands second generation caretaker Joseph Tibbs, surrounded by four bodies, one gripping onto his arms and swaying.

"Dear God! What happened here?" asks Paulie.

"Oh Paulie. You won't believe it." He points at the two men in the dirt, cloaked with mud. One has a jack hammer in his hand. The other still grips a cricket bat, standard issue.

"Those two men there were trying to take the marble from Mr. Leung's grave, I think. And you won't believe it, but I think your Michael and my boy Donovan stopped them."

"Michael?" whispers Paulie. He stares at the men coated in mud, one sprawled across the marble slab like he was sleeping in bed, the other still swaying, trying to hold his head high, mouth gaping.

"There you are," whispers Pao Pao. "Long time no see." And Pao Pao grabs the swaying man to her bosom. The man yields to her touch, hands falling flat to his sides. She runs her tender hands across the man's muddy head and whispers in his ear. And Paulie sees the young, muddy man nod, yes, yes, so fervently that mud runs off his face. Or are those tears? And even through the mud Paulie distinctly hears the boy murmur weakly in Pao Pao's ear yesyesohyesIsawhimIsawhim.

That there, mutters Paulie to himself, is another mystery perhaps solvable by a more patient, less hungry man.

"That there's my Donovan, Pao Pao," says Joseph. "Can't tell with all the mud."

"Glad to see you come," says Pao Pao, hugging Donovan tight. And now to business, thinks Pao Pao. She will clean these two boys up, her dear kin. They will pray properly, lighting their incense, bowing three times before offering their musky scent to the earth. And she will give them the whole bag of money to burn for the ancestors who listen when so inclined.

Things that were never known, that:

8. When patriarch Pa-Kung Leung first boarded his ship in Hong Kong, his mind was set for New York. Jamaica then was nothing to him, even as the dark mountain peaks rose coyly through the early morning mists as they sailed into Kingston Harbor. It was just another coastal, Caribbean town, with its markets and its slums and its endless noise. The ship had stopped at many such ports of call on its long serpentine journey. But the sea breeze was shifting, changing the course of his whole life as it blew right off his head the Panama hat he bought for too much money from some Punti in Hong Kong. As he rushed off-board to chase his brand new hat down Harbor Street, the wind of upheaval still hissing in his ears, he knew instantly he was never going to make it to New York. Not when the road felt so sound and certain under his feet — stronger than any promise of paradise.

Contributor Bios & Acknowedgments

Rosa Alcalá is the author of three books of poetry, most recently *MyOTHER TONGUE* (Futurepoem, 2017). Her poems appear in numerous anthologies and journals, including *Best American Poetry 2019*, *American Poets in the 21st Century: Poetics of Social Engagement*, *The Nation*, and *American Poetry Review*. The recipient of a National Endowment for the Arts Translation Fellowship, and runner-up for a PEN Translation Award, she is the editor and co-translator of *New & Selected Poems of Cecilia Vicuña* (Kelsey Street Press, 2018). She has given talks, readings, and workshops in both the U.S. and Latin America, and her poems have been, or are currently being, translated into Spanish, Portuguese, and Montenegrin. Originally from Paterson, NJ, she received her MFA in Creative Writing from Brown University and PhD in English from University at Buffalo. More about her here: rosaalcala.com

Sabahattin Ali was born in 1907 in the Ottoman town of Eğridere (now Ardino, in southern Bulgaria). A teacher, journalist, and poet, he owned and edited the popular satirical newspaper *Marko paşa*. A frequent target of government censorship, he was imprisoned twice for his writings and was killed on the Bulgarian border in 1948 as he attempted to flee Turkey. Today, Ali is an icon of social and political resistance among Turkish youth.

Kali Fajardo-Anstine is from Denver, Colorado. The author of *Sabrina & Corina*, a finalist for the National Book Award, the PEN/Bingham Prize, The Clark Prize, The Story Prize, and the Saroyan International Prize, as well as winner of an American Book Award, she is the 2021 recipient of the Addison M. Metcalf Award from the American Academy of Arts and Letters. She has written for *The New York Times*, *Harper's Bazaar*, *ELLE*, *O: the Oprah Magazine*, *The American Scholar*, *Boston Review*, and elsewhere, and has received fellowships from MacDowell, Yaddo, Hedgebrook, and Tin House. Fajardo-Anstine earned her MFA from the University of Wyoming and has lived across the country, from Durango, Colorado, to Key West, Florida. She is the 2022/23 Endowed Chair of Creative Writing at Texas State University. Her debut novel, *Woman of Light,* will be published in June, 2022.

Kianny N. Antigua is a fiction writer, poet and translator. She is a Senior Lecturer of Spanish at Dartmouth College, and an independent translator and adapter for Pepsqually VO Sound & Design, Inc. Antigua has published twenty-three books of children's literature, four of short stories, two collections of poems, two anthologies, a book of microfiction, a novel and a journal. She has won sixteen literary awards and many of her texts have been included in anthologies, literary magazines, newspapers and textbooks. Some have been translated into English, French and Italian. She is the translator (Eng./Spa.) and the audiobook narrator of *Dominicana* (Seven Stories Press, 2021) by Angie Cruz, translator of *Una niña rota con suerte* by Ruth Behar, & the YA novel *Nunca mires atrás* (Bloomsbury/Audible, 2022) by Lilliam Rivera.

Catalina Bartlett holds a PhD in English from Texas A&M University and an MFA from Indiana University. Her fiction has appeared in a previous issue of *Aster(ix)* and was nominated for a Pushcart Prize.

She has received a Ledig House Fellowship and an artist residency at Prairie Center for the Arts. She is an assistant professor in rhetoric and composition, a faculty fellow in Women and Gender Studies, and a core faculty member in both Digital Humanities and the Center for Latin American and Caribbean Studies at Michigan State University. She lives in Lansing, where she is at work on a short story collection that draws on her matrilineal family history and her early life along the southern Colorado-northern New Mexico corridor. To learn more about Catalina, visit: www.catalinabartlett.com.

Aysel K. Basci is a nonfiction writer and literary translator. She was born and raised in Cyprus and moved to the United States in 1975. Aysel is retired and resides in the Washington DC area. Her work has appeared in the *Michigan Quarterly Review, Adelaide Literary Magazine, Entropy, Bosphorus Review of Books* and elsewhere.

Jennifer Croft was awarded the Man Booker International Prize in 2018 and a National Book Award Finalist for her translation from Polish of Olga Tokarczuk's *FLIGHTS*. She is the recipient of Fulbright, PEN, MacDowell, and National Endowment for the Arts grants and fellowships, as well as the inaugural Michael Henry Heim Prize for Translation and a Tin House Workshop Scholarship for her memoir *HOMESICK*. She holds a PhD from Northwestern University and an MFA from the University of Iowa. She is a founding editor of *The Buenos Aires Review* and has published her own work and numerous translations in *The New York Times, The Los Angeles Review of Books, Granta, VICE, n+1, Electric Literature, Lit Hub, BOMB, Guernica, The New Republic, The Guardian, The Chicago Tribune,* and elsewhere. She currently divides her time between Buenos Aires and Los Angeles.

Hannah Eko is a Black-Nigerian writer, teaching artist, and creator of honeyknife, llc. Born in London, she grew up in Southern California and has lived on both sides of the ocean and some rivers in between. Her work has been featured in *Buzzfeed*, *Bust*, *b*tch*, *make/shift*, and a previous issue of *Aster(ix)* magazines. She is a 2019 recipient of the Advancing Black Arts Grant, a Peter R. Taylor Kenyon Fellow, Tin House Scholar, and VONA (Voices Of Our Nations) alum. She believes honey is the knife.

Racquel Goodison is on faculty at the Borough of Manhattan Community College. She has been a resident at Yaddo, Millay, and the Saltonstall Arts Colony. Additionally, she was a recipient of the Astraea Emerging Lesbian Writers Grant and the Archie D. and Bertha H. Walker Scholarship to the Fine Arts Works Center. Her stories, poems, and creative nonfiction have been nominated for the Pushcart and can be found in such literary journals as *Obsidian*, *Pleiades*, *Boston Review*, and *Drunken Boat*. Her chapbook, *Skin*, was a finalist for the 2013 Goldline Press Fiction Chapbook competition and the winner of the 2015 Creative Justice Press fiction chapbook competition. She is currently completing a collection of short stories.

Nathalie Handal is a poet, playwright, nonfiction and literary travel writer. She was raised in Latin America, France and the Middle East, and educated in Asia, the United States, and the United Kingdom. Her poetry collections are *Life in a Country Album*, *The Republics*, *Poet in Andalucía*, and *Love and Strange Horses*, winner of the Gold Medal Independent Publisher Book Award. She is the author of eight plays and editor of two anthologies including the groundbreaking classic *The Poetry of Arab Women: A Contemporary Anthology*, winner of the PEN Oakland Josephine Miles Book Award. She writes the literary travel column The City and the Writer for Words without Borders and resides in New York City. She is a professor at Columbia University, and a

Visiting Writer at the American University of Rome.

Mubanga Kalimamukwento's first novel, *The Mourning Bird* (Jacana Media), won the Dinaane Debut Fiction Award and was listed as one of The Top 15 Debut Books of 2019 by *Brittle Paper*. Mubanga won the Kalemba Short Story Prize, and her stories have since appeared on shortlists for the Bristol Short Story Prize, Nobrow Short Story Prize, and Dreamers Creative Writing. Her work has also been anthologized on Netflix and in various journals, including *Overland, Killens Review of Arts and Letters, The Red Rock Review*, and *The Menteur*. She was translated and published in Italian by *Menelique* and is an MFA candidate at Hamline University, where she received the Writer of Color Merit Scholarship and the Deborah Keenan Poetry Award. She is also a fiction editor at *Doek!*

Monique McIntosh is a short story writer originally from Kingston, Jamaica. Her fiction has been published in *Pleiades, Wasafiri Magazine, The Boiler Journal, Small Axe, Moko Magazine*, and *Bartleby Snopes*. Her short stories have been nominated for the Pushcart and Best of the Net prizes. She has an MFA in Creative Writing from Florida Atlantic University and a BA in English Literature from Davidson College. She currently lives in South Florida, where she writes about art and design.

Amy Olassa grew up in India, and currently lives in the Bay Area. She received her MFA in Creative Writing from Saint Mary's College of California. She is an alumna of the Community of Writers at Squaw Valley, the Tin House Workshop and was a 2018 Fellow at the SF Writer's Grotto. Her work was featured in the *Oyster River Pages* and nominated for the 2020 PEN/Robert J. Dau Short Story Prize for Emerging Writers.

Toni Margarita Plummer was born and raised in the San Gabriel Valley of Los Angeles, the daughter of a Mexican immigrant mother and white father. She is the author of the story collection *The Bolero of Andi Rowe* and was a finalist for the inaugural Tomás Rivera Book Prize. In 2019 she received Honorable Mention for the Reynolds Price Prize in Fiction given by the Center for Women Writers. A Macondo Fellow and graduate of the Master of Professional Writing Program at USC, she is a contributor to the anthologies *East of East: The Making of Greater El Monte* and *Latina Outsiders Remaking Latina Identity*. Plummer lives with her family in the Hudson Valley. You can find her on Twitter @tmargaritaplum.

Yolanda Arroyo Pizarro is a Puerto Rican writer. She's published books that promote the discussion of Afroidentity and sexual diversity. She is the Director of the Department of AfroPuertoRican Studies, a performative project of Creative Writing based at the Casa Museo Ashford in San Juan, Puerto Rico. She is also the founder and chair of Ancestral Black Women. She was invited by the UN to speak about women, slavery and creativity in 2015 as part of the Remembering Slavery Program. Her short story collection *Las negras* was winner of the 2013 National Short Story Prize from the PEN Club of Puerto Rico. She has also won the Institute of Puerto Rican Culture Prize in 2012 and 2015, and the National Award from the Institute of Puerto Rican Culture in 2008. Her work has been translated into French, German, Hungarian, Italian, and Portuguese.

Nelly A. Rosario is a Dominican-American author and creative writing instructor of *Song of the Water Saints*, winner of a PEN/Open Book Award. Her fiction and non-fiction works appear in various anthologies and journals. Rosario holds an MFA from Columbia University, where she has taught. She was formerly on faculty at Texas State University and a Visiting Scholar in the MIT Comparative Media Studies/Writing Program. Currently, Rosario is the 2017-18 Schumann Visiting Professor in Democratic Studies in the Latina/o Studies Program at Williams College and also serves as Assistant Director of Writing for the MIT Black History Project

Lawrence Schimel is a bilingual (Spanish/English) author and literary translator. His translations into English include *La Bastarda* by Trifonia Melibea Obono (The Feminist Press) and *Niños: Poems for the Lost Children of Chile* by María José Ferrada (Eerdmans); into Spanish, *Bluets* by Maggie Nelson (Tres Puntos Ediciones) and *Amesia Colectiva* by Koleka Putuma (with Arrate Hidalgo; Flores Raras).

Layhannara Tep was born and raised in Long Beach, California. She is the daughter of Cambodian refugees, an experience that continues to shape her writing. She is currently pursuing her master's in Asian American Studies at UCLA, where she is working on a collection of short stories about the Cambodian American diaspora. Layhannara enjoys stories and art in all forms. In her free time, you can find her at the movies, enjoying live music, or getting lost in a museum (she seriously gets lost everywhere). Layhannara enjoys ice cream on rainy days and iced coffees in any weather. She has a growing to-be-read pile. If you see her at a bookstore, please remind her she's not allowed to buy a new book until she finishes one she already owns. Seriously.

Acknowledgments

"Duvar (The Wall)" by Sabahattin Ali was originally published in 1936 in the journal Ayda Bir and later reproduced in his second book, Kağnı (1936, Oxcart).

"Quimbamba" by Yolanda Arroyo Pizarro was originally published in Spanish in 2018, self-published on Amazon as well as in the Afro-Hispanic Review (Volume 37, Number 1).

9 781942 547174